NO MATTER
WHAT HAPPENED,
SHE WOULD LOVE HIM . . .

She kissed his forehead, wishing that he would kiss her lips. When he didn't, she rubbed his back gently in the warm sun, as if he were a small child. For a long time, they just lay there together, holding each other until he stopped shaking.

At last he looked at her with a sad smile. "You really are my lovely," he said.

How lucky Melanie was to have had him propose, Joanna thought as they sat up and brushed the sand from their arms. She wondered if Melanie had even appreciated Matt's offer. What a terrible mess it all was. Yet she was glad that Matt had called her. She watched him reach into his pocket and pull out a pill bottle . . .

WHITHER THE WIND BLOWETH

ELAINE L. SCHULTE

AN AVON  FLARE BOOK

WHITHER THE WIND BLOWETH is an original publication of Avon Books. This work has never before appeared in book form.

Grateful acknowledgment is made to David Higham Associates Limited for copyrighted material.

Lines from "Morning Has Broken" in *The Children's Bells* by Eleanor Farjeon, Oxford University Press. Reprinted by permission.

AVON BOOKS
A division of
The Hearst Corporation
959 Eighth Avenue
New York, New York 10019

Copyright ©1982 by Elaine L. Schulte
Published by arrangement with the author
Library of Congress Catalog Card Number 82-1806
ISBN: 0-380-79384-9

Library of Congress Cataloging in Publication Data

Schulte, Elaine L.
  Whither the wind bloweth.
  (An Avon/Flare Book)
  Summary: Struggling to find acceptance in a new school, Joanna's life is complicated by a suicide, alcohol, and drugs until a brush with death turns her to Jesus.
  [1. Alcoholism—Fiction 2. Suicide—Fiction.
3. Conduct of life—Fiction. 4. Christian life—Fiction] I. Title.
PZ7.S3367Wh   [Fic]   82-1806
ISBN 0-380-79384-9 (pbk.)   AACR2

First Flare Printing, September, 1982

FLARE BOOKS TRADEMARK REG. U. S. PAT. OFF. AND IN OTHER COUNTRIES, MARCA REGISTRADA, HECHO EN U. S. A.

Printed in the U. S. A.

WFH 10 9 8 7 6 5 4 3 2 1

Broken wings can soar again;
   shattered voices can sing anew,
   with wondrous beauty, unknown before.

CHAPTER 1

Something terrible is going to happen, Joanna Stevens thought as she waited alone at the school bus stop. Shifting her armload of books, she peeled off her brown cardigan, and the sun was immediately hot against her arms. It felt like a bad omen, such heat at seven on Halloween morning.

Maybe it was the hot wind whipping through the eucalyptus trees that frightened her, she thought. The towering trees reeled like crazed dancers against the cloudless blue California sky, branches bending and silvery green leaves fluttering wildly.

Devil winds. Santa Anas. She had read about them. They swept fires across Southern California every fall, bringing out arsonists and other crazies. Some people said that Santa Anas brought on suicides.

Strange. Back home in Kansas, people were expecting winter. Here in Santa Rosita, people expected fires and suicides!

The gusting wind muffled the sound of a car until it stopped in front of her. She looked up, amazed. Matt Thompson sat grinning widely at her from his bright red Corvette.

What is he doing here? she wondered, pulling back windblown wisps of her brown hair. Matt lived way over by the ocean, on the other side of Santa Rosita. Why would he drive here?

He leaned across the seat as he opened the door for

her. "Joanna, my lovely, I was in the neighborhood and knew you were dying to go to school." He grinned. "Want a ride?"

"Sure, thanks." She smiled at his come-on and hopped in. Everyone knew that Matt was forever trying to be a swinger, so what had prompted him to stop by for her? He was tall, thin, a sun-bleached blond, and dreamily handsome—a popular senior, very big on campus. She was an unknown junior, new here from Kansas. She had hoped that he would notice her since the first day of school.

"If you're wondering why I'm in the neighborhood," he said with a straight face, "I had an important medical consultation. I'm a world-renowned expert on heart palpitations, you know."

"Really, Dr. Thompson," she said, trying not to laugh. She had seen Matt in a starlight community play in August—he could act, he could sing, he could dance. What's more, he was a top student and captain of last year's winning basketball team. But an expert on heart palpitations?

He was staring straight at her, completely serious.

"Really!" she said again, and before she knew what had happened, he was kissing her.

Astonished, she pushed him away, catching her breath, not knowing what to say.

He sat back and inhaled deeply, rolling his green eyes and holding a hand over his heart. "Now that's what I call heart palpitations," he said.

She couldn't help laughing. No one could help liking Matt and his crazy humor. Quite a few girls at school were madly in love with him. Anyhow, it wasn't a serious kiss. There was no sense in trying to fool herself. It was only part of his constantly changing act.

"Well," he said, grinning at her, "onward to school. We'll teach the teachers what's what."

Joanna saw her neighbor David Porter, hurrying

8

down the road toward the school bus stop. "Maybe we should give David a ride. It's so hot."

"No way, my lovely. No way!" Matt expertly maneuvered his Corvette onto the street, leaving a trail of gray dust. "He's one of those religious nuts."

She waved quickly at David, and he waved back through the dust. He looked surprised to see her with Matt Thompson. Everyone would be!

"You know, my lovely, I'm going to put you in the movies. I have connections. I'll make you a star."

"I'll bet," she said. She had heard that his mother had been in the movies, but surely he was just kidding. "Do you say that to all of the girls?" she asked.

He smiled, watching her more than his driving.

She wished that he would keep his eyes on the road instead of on her. All he could see anyway was a small brunette with big brown eyes. People said she was pretty, but she wasn't so sure about it.

"Wondering what I have in mind, eh?" he asked, grinning at her like a villain.

"You're crazy!"

"You've got it!" He grabbed her hand and kissed it loudly, over and over. "Would you like to go with me to Melanie Tillinghast's party tonight?" he asked between kisses.

She laughed. She could hardly believe this: Matt Thompson, kissing her hand like some mad comedian, and, at last, her chance to be part of Melanie's group—the popular kids, just as she had been in Kansas all through school. "Sure. I'd like to." She hoped that she didn't sound too anxious.

His act continued all the way to school. She hadn't laughed so much since she moved to Santa Rosita in August.

When they pulled up in the school parking lot, three of Matt's friends yelled, waving him over. How surprised they were to see her with him.

Others in the parking lot turned toward them as if the word were spreading. Who could miss any girl whom Matt might drive around in that bright red Corvette! She tried not to look too pleased.

In the distance someone said, "Leave it to old Matt to check out the newest chick. We've got to move faster."

"Yeah, but he never gets himself tied down," someone else said.

She glanced at Matt, wondering if he had heard. He was smiling, and his green eyes did not meet hers. It seemed like a warning: not to count too seriously on him.

"See you tonight at seven-thirty," he said, sliding out of the Corvette gracefully for someone so tall.

"Okay." She let herself out.

"I'll be ready," she called after him, but he didn't seem to hear. He was heading for his friends, yelling about the weekend weather for a sailing trip to Catalina Island.

She smiled at the kids who glanced at her. Everyone would know that she had a date with Matt Thompson. Maybe she wasn't popular yet at Santa Rosita, but Matt was the first step. Melanie's party was the second. The day felt as exciting as the strange hot wind.

Heading up the leafy stairs toward the Spanish-style school, she began to feel at home. She glanced at the white stucco buildings with their red tile roofs. They had been built years ago and seemed foreign to her at first. Now they felt just right. After two terribly lonely months, she was becoming a real part of Santa Rosita High!

She recalled telling her mother about the three groups at school. There was a popular group, who seemed a lot wilder than the kids back in Kansas. And there were the boozers and stoners, who had

10

burned out their brains with alcohol or drugs. Then there was the big crowd of kids in the middle.

Strange, she thought. In Kansas she had been a cheerleader, class vice-president, secretary of the student council, honor roll student . . . and popular. Here she was part of the big middle group—entirely out of it.

She hurried through the crowd for her outdoor locker. She would not be "out of it" much longer! Not after Melanie's party. Matt's invitation was even better than her best daydreams.

As she pulled her American lit. book from her locker, she remembered that she hadn't asked Matt what to wear. After all, it was Halloween. Maybe they were supposed to wear costumes.

She stood biting her lip, then recalled that Melanie was usually around the French classroom first period. Slamming her locker, Joanna rushed to find her.

Melanie was just coming around the corner, surrounded by three of her friends. She looked tan and beautiful, as cool as a fashion model. Her long black hair was coiled loosely around her head. Thick black lashes encircled her violet eyes, which had just a hint of mysterious dark smudges beneath them.

Did she wear violet contact lenses? Joanna wondered. The color was distracting. And she thought that Melanie's matching violet sundress would have been outlawed in Kansas schools.

She stood on tiptoe to call over the crowd. "Melanie?"

Melanie glanced toward Joanna, then away to her friends.

After making her way through the crowd by the French classroom, Joanna arrived at the door just as Melanie turned to go in. "Melanie . . ." She reached out to touch her shoulder.

Melanie turned indignantly.

"Matt invited me to your party tonight, and he didn't say if we should wear Halloween costumes or what—"

"Matt's bringing *you?*" She made it sound as if she couldn't imagine why Matt would ask her. She glanced at her friends, who stood coolly inspecting Joanna.

For a long moment Joanna couldn't think what to say. "I hope that's all right," she finally stammered.

Melanie smiled haughtily. "Well, it's not a children's party, you know. You could wear that costume you have on now." She turned and stalked into the classroom with her smiling friends behind her.

Joanna felt the stares of nearby students. She turned away, her face flaming, and headed for American lit. Sudden tears stung her eyes and clung to her lashes. She willed herself not to break down sobbing.

Perhaps Melanie is right about this outfit, she thought. It had been perfect last year in Kansas, just the kind of thing the teen magazines showed: brown and gold plaid skirt, gold blouse, and brown cardigan.

But teen magazine clothes didn't really fit in at Santa Rosita. Nothing she did seemed to fit in. Nothing! She wished that her family had never moved to California!

She bit down on her lower lip as it trembled, but it didn't stop her burst of tears.

CHAPTER 2

Joanna hurried across the school patio to the portable building for American lit. The only good thing about the wind, she decided, was that it quickly dried tears.

She glanced around. Everyone was too busy with his or her own life. No one noticed her at all. No one even cared. Worst of all, she still didn't know if she was supposed to wear a costume to Melanie's party.

The hot wind buffeted bursts of red bougainvillaea blooming across the old white walls. If only this wind would stop, she thought as dry blossoms and leaves rustled across the sidewalk. It made her feel edgy. Was it the wind that made Melanie edgy, too?

Well, it wasn't worth crying about anyhow, she told herself firmly. She was not going to let Melanie spoil the day or her date with Matt.

She headed for her classroom.

"Hey, Joanna!" someone called from the back row as she stepped into the room.

She turned. It was Chad Chandler, one of Matt's friends and co-captain of the football team. "Hi," she said.

He grinned, then turned to some of his friends, no doubt spreading the news of her ride with Matt . . . and maybe about their date tonight. None of Matt's friends seemed to have noticed her before.

She sat down in her front-row seat. Maybe she

could switch to a seat in the back. All the popular kids sat back there.

Heidi Matthias plopped an armload of books onto the desk next to Joanna's. "Missed you on the bus."

"I had a ride," Joanna said, hoping that Heidi would ask who had picked her up.

Heidi lifted her long blond hair away from her tan neck. "It's so hot today! I thought maybe these Santa Anas were too much for you, and you were still under the covers."

"No. Not quite." Joanna thought that was just where she would like to have been when Melanie snapped at her. "It's weird, though, to have hot weather at Halloween."

"Devil winds." Heidi slid into her seat. "Devil winds and Halloween. Sounds like bad spirits running amuck."

Joanna couldn't resist telling her. "Matt Thompson's invited me to Melanie's party tonight."

Heidi look startled. "Bad spirits all right."

"What do you mean?"

Heidi looked sorry. "I should think before I talk. But, seriously, watch out for Melanie. She's like a wild mustang that doesn't take to taming—"

"Should I wear a costume to Melanie's party?" Joanna interrupted. She didn't want to hear Heidi's usual talk about horses. And she didn't want to hear any criticism about Matt's friends.

Heidi shrugged. "Better ask Matt. They'll laugh at you if you're the only one in costume . . . or they'll laugh if they're all wearing costumes and you're not. I don't know what's in with them nowadays."

Joanna felt uncertain. She did not want them laughing at her.

"The only thing I know for sure is that their rules are always changing," Heidi added. "You have to be fast on your feet to stay on that track."

Joanna wasn't surprised. She glanced out the door thoughtfully. The kids passing by struggled against the wind just as she had been struggling to fit in at this school. The wind whipped their hair, shirts, and skirts until everyone looked unreal. Today everything seemed so strange.

"I've never really thought of people being like horses."

Heidi looked a bit embarrassed. "I guess I do a lot. You know, plow horses, quarter horses, thoroughbreds, and beautiful wild mustangs . . . like Melanie."

"Yes. I guess I can see her a little like that," Joanna decided.

"Wild mustangs are beautiful, but they don't fit in well among people." Heidi looked away. "I guess I'd rather be a thoroughbred."

Joanna knew what she meant—a strong, kind person. She laughed. "What am I, a plow horse?"

"No. Not at all." Heidi smiled thoughtfully as she dug her American lit. book out of her orange backpack. "I'm not sure yet about you. You haven't settled in," she said with a little laugh as the class bell rang.

Opening her lit. book, Joanna wished that she could be more like Heidi in some ways. Heidi knew her goal: to go to the best vet college in the country. Most of the other juniors were thinking about college already, too.

She sighed quietly. Right now she'd have to forget about her future and about Matt and Melanie. Right now she'd better concentrate on this class. Mrs. Ekelman was already discussing Edgar Allan Poe's "The Cask of Amontillado." Poe, Joanna thought, had been a crazy genius. Like Matt.

At lunchtime Matt stopped by her locker.

"Joanna, my lovely!" he exclaimed as if he were amazed to find her there. "Come along to see old Matt's noontime performance."

She subdued a giggle as he grabbed her hand and hurried her to the patio next to the auditorium. It was protected from the wind, and everyone was congregating there. People turned, surprised to see them together, but she pretended not to notice.

"Madam," he said, bowing her onto a patio bench with a great flourish.

Melanie arrived in her daring violet sundress. "Well, here I am," she said. "This had better be good."

Matt beamed. "It is! It is!" He escorted her to the bench beside Joanna with the same grand flourish.

Joanna and Melanie smiled uncertainly at each other, but Matt was already beginning his act—a wild macho imitation of Mr. Zale, the football coach.

A crowd gathered, laughing in appreciation.

Matt seemed to become Mr. Zale, strutting around like him, imitating his voice to perfection as he bellowed out orders.

He is funny, Joanna thought. She glanced at Melanie.

Melanie's mind seemed far away on something grim. Her hands were tightly clenched in the lap of her violet dress.

"Isn't he a riot?" Joanna asked, then saw the hard glaze of anger in Melanie's eyes as she turned.

Melanie forced a little smile. "Yes. Matt's a riot." Her eyes softened for a moment. "Matt's okay." She said it as if she were his older sister.

For a moment Joanna hoped that they could be friends.

Two of Melanie's friends stopped by, calling her, and the moment passed. Applauding Matt, Melanie dipped a theatrical little bow and started toward her friends.

Joanna had a feeling that Melanie and Matt played these little theatrical acts often. She watched Melanie hurrying away, noticing how cool and sophisticated she looked. From what everyone said, Melanie did a lot of fashion modeling for photographers in Los Angeles.

Joanna turned back to Matt's performance. Quite a crowd had gathered; they roared with laughter as Matt imitated Mr. Zale trying to dance to rock.

Later, while the fun of Matt's act still lingered and everyone was drifting away, Joanna asked, "Am I supposed to wear a costume to the Halloween party?"

Matt glanced at her sharply, as if he couldn't believe her words. "No way! No way! And it's not a Halloween party. Melanie doesn't have anything that common. You would be the laughingstock."

"I'd be a disaster," Joanna answered breezily. Despite his smile, she knew from the look in his green eyes that she had better not be an embarrassment to him tonight at the party. Matt was serious. She would have to be careful of what she said.

That afternoon, as she waited in the school bus crowd, she wondered if Matt would stop by to give her a ride home. She pressed against the wind, holding down her brown plaid skirt—her costume, as Melanie had called it. Yet since they had watched Matt together during lunch hour, some of the sting had gone out of Melanie's words. She wondered if he had hoped for their being friendly.

Where was he? She finally got on the bus. It would be such a dull ride home. Heidi took a different bus home on Fridays so she could help at the animal care center.

"Hey, Joanna!"

She glanced up. It was David Porter, her neighbor, sitting near the middle of the bus.

"Hey, I saved a seat for you!"

He was so loud that she couldn't ignore him. He was a nice guy, but as Matt had said, he was a religious nut. He was a sophomore, kind of cute but gawky. He looked as if he'd grown so quickly that he couldn't figure out what to do with his arms and legs.

He was standing up to give her the window seat. His blond, wavy hair was windblown, and his glasses had slipped halfway down his nose. "I'm glad you're coming home on the bus," he said, seeming unaware that the kids at the back of the bus were laughing at him.

Maybe he thought that Matt had lost interest in her already. David had seen Matt pick her up. "Yes, well, Matt has to get going on arrangements for a party tonight."

David blinked hard, looking at her strangely.

"Thanks for the seat," she finally said.

They glanced out the window in silence. Suddenly she saw him—Matt in his bright red Corvette. Worse, Melanie was with him! They were stopped, waiting for traffic to pass.

Joanna couldn't take her eyes away from them. She saw Matt look with a terrible yearning at Melanie as he asked her something. Melanie turned to him with an indignant look, as if to say, Don't be ridiculous!

Joanna quickly turned away, then saw the concern in David's eyes. She tried to smile off the whole scene. "The party tonight is at Melanie's, you know. Matt will be helping her get things ready. They've been friends since before first grade."

David smiled kindly. "You don't have to worry about her. She doesn't go out with younger fellows." He was quiet for a moment. "That's not gossip either. She says she won't go out with anyone under twenty-five."

"You're kidding!" That was crazy, she thought.

18

"Well, she's almost nineteen. She lost a half year of school when she lived in Europe. She graduates in January."

"Who told you she doesn't date anyone under twenty-five?"

"When high school kids ask her out, that's what she tells them. She said the same thing to a couple of college guys, including my cousin."

"Maybe it's just a kind way of letting them down." She watched Matt's car take off through the parking lot traffic and roar down to the road.

"I don't know," David said. "I heard she's mad about a famous golf pro in L.A."

"How on earth would she get to know a famous golf pro?"

David's face was suddenly red. "He used to date her mother."

Her mother! Joanna watched the red Corvette disappear down the road. She had heard amazing stories about Melanie's mother. She had been divorced four times! Someone had called her the playgirl of Santa Rosita Hills.

David was certainly embarrassed about the whole subject, she thought as the bus finally took off. She glanced at him sideways.

His eyes were closed, his long lashes dark against his fair skin. As he opened his eyes and saw her watching, a blush rose again on his face. "I hope you have a kind way of letting boys down, too . . . because . . . Well, this is really last-minute. Anyhow, I wondered if you'd go to a senior high church party with me tomorrow night. Actually I mean, come to the party at my house with me."

Joanna knew she didn't dare smile. He sounded so confused. Maybe it was the first time he'd ever asked a girl for a date! What could she say? She didn't want to hurt him, but she didn't want to go. Perhaps Matt would ask her out if he didn't go sailing.

19

David was still smiling. "You just have to say no if you don't want to go."

"I do want to," she found herself saying, "but I'll probably be busy."

"Yeah," he said. "I figured you'd rather go out with Matt. It's okay."

It didn't look okay at all. He looked crushed. "Actually it depends on the weather. Matt may be sailing this weekend." She remembered overhearing him talk about it this morning in the school parking lot.

David brightened. "Oh, the weather will be great for sailing. But I'll call you tomorrow morning."

"Okay." She sat back, and they looked uneasily at each other.

"Is it a costume party?" she asked. This time she would find out right away!

"No. Just a party. Actually our church doesn't go for Halloween parties with witches and devils and all of that."

Did they think that there was something bad about witch and devil costumes? She had never even considered that. Maybe he belonged to a weird church or even to a cult!

"Why don't you wear those kinds of costumes?" she asked.

"It doesn't make sense for Christians to get involved with celebrating a night given to witches and demons."

"I guess I can understand that," Joanna said. She recalled her grandfather telling her about God and Jesus when she was little. Sometimes now she wondered if the memory was only her imagination. Anyhow, she would rather talk about something else. Religion was for little kids and old people.

"Tell me about the party," she said.

David looked pleased to be asked. "It's just a monthly party. We have parties or trips to Disneyland or go to movies or something every month. Last summer we went to Alaska on a mission."

A mission! Was he a missionary?

"What's it like in Alaska?" she finally asked, hoping to divert his attention from any missionary talk.

The rest of the bus ride home he told her about Alaska—about great humpbacked whales, sea lions, glaciers, and icebergs. It sounded as if they had fun, but then he didn't discuss the missionary part of it.

He was still telling her about their adventures in Alaska when they stepped off the bus into the hot gusting wind. They walked up the leaf-littered blacktop road to the hillside development of new Spanish houses. As they reached Joanna's driveway, he laughed at himself. "Afraid I really got wound up."

"It was interesting," she said to be polite, although she hadn't really been bored. "Good-bye, David."

"I'll call you," he said.

She headed for the black wrought-iron gate in the white wall around her backyard. A strange feeling made her turn to the road above that wound up to David's house. He had stopped and was looking down at her. She thought for a moment that he was praying.

They both waved and turned away.

She kicked at the eucalyptus bark and twigs whirling at her feet. It had turned out to be a good day despite the devil winds and her early-morning premonition.

What would her family think about Matt? And what would Matt think of her family? She wanted everthing to be perfect. She opened the gate leading to the backyard and the Mexican tile patio.

Shaded by the patio table's yellow umbrella, her father and a strange man sat in the colorful webbed chairs. "Hi, baby!" her father shouted out to her. He stood up, grinning crookedly, then reeled and was laughing. "Come on," he sputtered, "meet my new friend." He staggered and sat down hard in the webbed chair.

Joanna forced a polite smile at the stranger. He looked bedraggled, as if he had been picked up out of an alley. But so did her father. They both were drunk, terribly drunk.

How could he do this again? she thought bitterly. He had been sober for more than a year! He had promised that he wouldn't drink if they moved to California.

Her mind raced as she walked slowly toward them. Cathy would be home on the grade school bus in half an hour! She shouldn't see Dad like this! Their mother wouldn't be home from work until five-thirty. Oh, why did he have to ruin everything!

There was an empty liquor bottle in a planter box and a half-empty bottle on the table near their drinking glasses. The wind whipped Joanna's hair across her face, reminding her of her premonition. She had known something terrible would happen today.

"Joanna, baby," her father was saying, "this is my friend—" He laughed, his handsome face red and blotchy. "Wass your name?"

She did not want to believe that this was her father. He usually looked so handsome, so neatly dressed for his job as a computer salesman. But now his graying hair was wild, his white shirt rumpled, and his blue eyes were red and watery.

"Pretty little thing," the man said. "I'm partial to brunettes with big brown eyes."

Joanna backed away. She could hear the phone ringing inside. "I'd better answer the phone. Excuse me."

Relieved, she whirled and ran for the back door,

which she slammed behind her. Grabbing the kitchen phone, she gasped, "Hello."

"Joanna! I hoped you'd be home," her mother said. "Do you know where Dad is? His office called me here, trying to locate him."

She could see the two men through the window. If only she could wish all this away. If only she didn't have to tell her mother!

"Joanna?" Her mother asked with a note of alarm.

Joanna took a deep breath. "He's drunk."

She was empty, detached, as if this time it were happening to someone else's family. "He and some—some man, out on the patio . . ." She felt like crying. "Oh, Mom, I finally have a date tonight with Matt Thompson. He's picking me up at seven-thirty!"

There was a long silence, and she felt embarrassed. She was putting her date first. She was being selfish, more concerned about herself than her whole family. But if only they knew what a dream Matt was.

Her mother's words were flat and serious. "Lock yourself into your room. I'll be home in fifteen minutes."

The memory of her father in a drunken rage, slapping her face hard, made her rush to her room and lock the door. She tried to push the bad memories away. She did not want to remember.

She went to the open window.

Hot air blasted down the dry hills to the house. She closed the window quietly and drew the leafy green and white draperies. It was a relief not to hear the wind.

She stood still, absorbing the quiet, the serene silence.

It was such a beautiful room, she thought, trying to concentrate on that. White walls and dark beams

23

on the ceiling. The leafy grean and white bedspreads on the twin beds matched the draperies, even the wallpaper in her adjoining bathroom.

The decorator had sold them the hanging baskets of ferns and the potted plants in their Mexican containers. The room looked like a garden with a fluffy white carpet. Joanna had hoped that life here would be as lovely as her room. She closed her eyes. They would have to hide her father's drinking problem again.

What if Mom had to quit her new job? Her mother couldn't just stay home taking care of Dad. They had spent so much money buying this model home with the furniture and everything in it, not to mention her father's new Buick. Her mother had to work now, although she seemed to like her job as an executive secretary at an electronics company.

Well, she had better tidy her room, Joanna decided. At least it would be done for tomorrow. Saturday was cleaning day. She picked up clothes, organized skirts and slacks and blouses in her closet, and straightened the bookshelf wall. How could time pass so slowly? If only she could see the driveway from her window.

She thought she heard a car door slam. Moments later her mother was whispering at the door. "Joanna?"

She opened the door.

Her mother's face, white and pinched, looked older. Her brown eyes were pale with worry. Tendrils of brown hair had escaped her upswept hairdo. "I want you to go out the front door and take my car. Here's money and a grocery list. I want you to pick up Cathy at the school bus stop and take her to buy those white moccasins she's been wanting."

Joanna stared blankly at the keys and the list. Last week her mother had told Cathy that they couldn't afford the moccasins. This was just an excuse to keep Cathy out of the house.

"Hurry! And don't come home until five o'clock," her mother said. "That will give you time to get ready for your date."

She felt her mother propel her toward the front door.

"And don't tell Cathy. Or anyone else."

"Okay, Mom." Joanna suddenly kissed her. "I'm sorry . . . I'm so sorry."

"It has nothing to do with you, honey. Now go!"

Joanna rushed for the front door and out into the hot wind. Her mother's wood-paneled station wagon was already turned around. She had thought out even that.

As Joanna drove down to the school bus stop, she wondered if her mother had been arranging life around her father's drinking problem all these years. Probably. She remembered her parents fighting in Kansas, her mother's black eyes, her father throwing her across the room. . . . She'd hated him so!

She made her mind stop. They were ugly memories she had managed to hide away during this one good year.

Well, she wouldn't ever let Cathy know. Ugly memories were too hard to forget.

Pulling up near the bus stop, she saw Cathy's yellow school bus in the distance. She turned off the ignition and glanced back up the hill toward her house.

Leaves and branches littered the road curving up the hillside. Some of the Spanish-style houses in the forty-house subdivision were almost hidden by the wildly blowing eucalyptus trees. Her house, halfway up the hill, white and lovely with its red tile roof, looked as serene as her room. The white stucco wall curved around the back patio.

25

For the first time she felt grateful for the wall. Whatever was going on now in her backyard was hidden.

The school bus braked to a stop, and its doors flapped open. Cathy was first off the bus. Her brown eyes opened wide with delight when she saw Joanna. Cathy's best friend, Dede, was right behind her.

From a distance they looked almost like twins— except that Cathy was a bit shorter than and not as skinny as Dede. Both of them had brown hair cut in bangs and braided into fat pigtails. And both wore white blouses and pink jeans. The only difference in their outfits was their shoes. Dede wore her white moccasins.

Now Cathy would have hers, too. Joanna hoped that Cathy would never know why. Leaning over to open the car door, she called, "Cathy! We're going shopping for your moccasins."

Cathy's brown eyes sparkled with surprise. "Really?"

"Yep." She couldn't help smiling, Cathy looked so pleased.

Cathy turned to Dede. "I'm really going to get them!" She hopped into the car. "I'll call you when I get home!"

"Did you have a good day?" Joanna asked as they pulled onto the main road behind the bright yellow school bus. She was determined to divert Cathy's attention from why she had been picked up at the bus stop. There was no need for Cathy to ever know what was happening at home.

CHAPTER 3

Just after five o'clock Joanna and Cathy stepped into the house. Serene stereo music swirled through the air as they made their way with the groceries through the Mexican tile entry and family room. There was no sign of their father or the other man.

In the kitchen their mother turned to smile at them as she put an apple cobbler into the oven. She had let down her long brown hair and brushed it. She looked much younger, but her brown eyes were dull. She seemed subdued. Had she taken tranquilizers?

Cathy rushed into her mother's arms. "Thank you for my moccasins!" She pointed a foot to show them off, then gave her mother another hug. "I didn't think I'd get any."

She kissed the top of Cathy's head. "Don't be too loud, dear. Your father was so tired that he went to bed."

How had she managed that? Joanna wondered. Had she slipped him some of her tranquilizers?

She put her bags of groceries down on the white counter. If only Dad would sleep through the night! If only she could get away without introducing him to Matt tonight. Well, she was not even going to think about it.

"Aren't you going to tell us how you happen to have a date with the famous Matt Thompson?" her mother asked as they put away groceries. She had seen him in the starlight community play, too.

Joanna found herself beginning to cheer up as she

told them about Matt picking her up at the bus stop and his invitation to Melanie Tillinghast's party.

"You mean you're going to the Tillinghast house?" her mother asked. "Well, I almost wish that I could go to your party. You know, their house was featured in a national architectural digest. They have all sorts of benefit parties. Famous people come there to raise money for charities."

Were they that rich? Joanna wondered uneasily. They lived "behind the gates." That meant there were security men guarding the gated private roads into Santa Rosita Hills. Her parents had looked at a few houses there with a realtor, but it was far too expensive.

Matt's family had lived in Santa Rosita Hills all his life until last year, Heidi had told her. After his parents' divorce they had sold the house, and he and his father had moved to the beach. His mother and two sisters had moved to Palm Springs. His mother had married again—this time to a much younger man.

"You'll have to give me a report on the house," her mother was saying, "although I expect my curiosity will kill me with envy." She laughed. "Maybe you'd better not tell me about it!"

"Oh, Mom, we have the most beautiful house in the world," Cathy said. "Anyhow, I love it. And I love you!" She hugged her mother hard, as if she had sensed something was wrong that had nothing at all to do with the elegance of the Tillinghast house.

After supper Joanna rushed to her room, glad that her father wasn't awake yet.

She would wear her new white crinkled Mexican dress with the big yellow flowers and green leaves embroidered across the front. She had bought it with her birthday money the Sunday her family drove across the border for their first look at Mexico.

She carefully pulled the dress out from the back of her closet. It was perfect for tonight; it was just what girls here would wear. Long, but cotton and casual. A California patio dress.

An hour later she was looking at herself in the full-length mirror in her bedroom. With her long brown hair freshly washed and blown dry, her tan, and the new Mexican dress down to her white sandals, she finally looked just like a California girl. She smiled at her reflection.

Cathy knocked at the door, then peeked in. "He's here, Joanna! Matt Thompson's here! He thought he told you seven o'clock."

"Shhh!" Joanna whispered in a panic. "We'd better not wake up Dad!"

Cathy glanced at her curiously.

"Go tell Matt I'm coming," she said, although it wasn't necessary. She grabbed her white Mexican string handbag and was on Cathy's heels in the hallway.

She thought she heard her father rattle the doorknob of her parents' room, then mutter groggily. Had her mother locked him in? she wondered as she hurried down the hall. Oh, please, please don't come out and spoil everything!

Matt and her mother were in the family room in front of the TV. The evening news blared out, but they seemed oblivious to it. Her mother was beaming. Matt had already charmed her.

"Hi," Joanna said, interrupting them.

Matt turned and stopped in the middle of his sentence. "Wow, you look beautiful," he said, then thoughtfully added, "You know, you look like your mother."

"Thank you, sir." She glanced at her mother. How pleased she looked. Well, he certainly knew how to get the better of mothers! "You look beautiful, too," Joanna teased.

He laughed. He was wearing a tan T-shirt and brown corduroy shorts.

She looked down in despair at her long white Mexican dress. "I'm dressed all wrong," she said, not realizing it until that moment.

"Perhaps you'd better change, Joanna," her mother suggested. "What should Joanna wear?" she asked Matt.

"That's perfect." He turned to go. "The girls wear things like that."

Anxious to rush out before her father stumbled in, she hoped Matt was being honest about what the girls wore. There was no time to change.

She edged him to the front door as he talked politely with her mother and Cathy. He knew how to charm even little girls, Joanna thought. Cathy's big brown eyes sparkled with delight as she looked up at him.

She thought she heard her father down the hallway. "We'd better go, Matt."

He almost looked as if he didn't want to leave. Was he acting again? Maybe. Although with his mother and two little sisters in Palm Springs . . .

Matt tugged Cathy's fat brown pigtails, and she giggled. From the wistful look in his eyes as he laughed, Joanna felt certain. Matt hadn't been acting at all. He missed being around a real family.

"Forgot my wallet," he said with a rueful smile as they walked out to his red Corvette. "We'll have to swing by my house. We have plenty of time anyhow."

"Sure." She wondered if he would help her in the car door, but he didn't. His thoughts seemed far away, as though something were very wrong.

They were on the main road before he glanced at her. "Hello there, my lovely! It's Friday night, and we're going to celebrate!"

30

Joanna laughed, relieved. She had escaped without her father's ruining everything for her with Matt. She had escaped! She felt wonderfully carefree. She was not even going to think about her father tonight!

"You'll have a chance to meet Rena," Matt said.

"Who's Rena?"

"Our house-sitter when Dad's out of town. Anyway, that's what he calls her. I'm supposed to be too old for baby-sitters. You know, she cooks and waits for repairmen and oversees the cleaning lady."

Sounds like a substitute mother, Joanna thought. She wondered if that had ever occurred to Matt.

On the way to his house Matt, crazy again, acted his way through what had happened to him and Melanie since kindergarten. They had gone to school camps together, riding and tennis camps. They even had the same piano teachers and recitals.

They sounded almost like a brother and sister, Joanna thought. Yet she couldn't help feeling jealous.

As they pulled up to Matt's beach house in the darkness, Joanna was amazed. She expected a beach cottage, a battered bachelor pad for just Matt and his father. Instead, spotlights illuminated an ultramodern white structure that looked as if it had landed from outer space. There were porthole windows and roofs slanting from all angles. A white wrought-iron fence surrounded the yard, making the effect even more stark against the night sky.

Tall palm trees, their green fronds all but snapping in gusts of wind, did not make the house seem any more real.

She sat there so long staring at the house that Matt came around to let her out of the car.

"I guess it doesn't look much like a Kansas house," he said.

31

"Oh, they have modern houses there, too," she protested, hoping that she didn't seem too stupid. "I've just never been in one."

The hot wind swept back her hair, and it occurred to her that this house seemed more suited to a desert than next to the Pacific Ocean. "It's very beautiful," she said, although that wasn't quite the right word. *Unusual* was more like it.

They walked in through the back door, stepping into a white and black kitchen with gleaming stainless steel cabinets, refrigerator, and counters. The kitchen felt eerie. Cold. Not like anything she had ever seen except in magazines. Her eyes were drawn to a basket of oranges, lemons, and limes for their warm colors.

"This way," Matt said, leading the way through the middle of the very white house to the enormous front entry with its carved double doors. A white metal staircase curved upstairs through the two-story entry. "Just make yourself at home," he said, starting up the stairs.

"Thanks."

She glanced around the entry hall. Above the double doors there was a great round window, a huge porthole. It seemed perfect here with the muffled roar of the ocean always in the house. But the house did not feel like a home.

Joanna walked over to a bench and sat down uneasily in the middle of the long canvas cushion.

She glanced at the enormous oil painting behind her. It rose halfway into the second floor of the entry. Mostly white, the painting had swirls of lavender and purple spiraling into mustard green dots. Expensive, she thought. Beautiful in a haunting way.

Straight ahead she saw the white living room lit by spotlights and white plastic lamps, the shades of which were shaped like mushrooms. Steel and glass tables held lamps and glass ashtrays among the white leather and plastic furniture. Stainless steel mobiles dangled in museumlike splendor between huge abstract paintings.

It was taking Matt a long time to find his wallet. She stood up and wandered to the living room, then came to an abrupt stop. A whole wall was really a great window overlooking the ocean. Floodlights lit the huge dark waves rolling in across the distant sand.

It was a few moments before Joanna noticed the older blond woman in the white dress reading near the far side of the window. "Oh, I'm sorry," Joanna said, backing away.

The woman turned to her and stood up with a slow smile. "You must be Matt's friend," she said, putting down her book and coming to her.

"Yes."

"I'm Rena," she said softly, extending a hand.

Rena's eyes seemed to engulf Joanna. How beautiful she was. She was older than her mother, but how young her eyes made her look.

"I'm Joanna."

Rena was still holding her hand. "I know. I know a great deal about you."

How could she? Joanna wondered. Matt didn't know much about her.

His footsteps pounded down the stairs; then he was behind them, stuffing his wallet in his pocket. "I guess you two have met. We'd better get going."

As they left, Joanna turned and found Rena watching her. "It was nice meeting you."

Rena smiled. "Maybe Matt will let me cook dinner for both of you some night."

"Good idea," Matt said. "I'll take you up on that. See you later."

As they stepped outside, he said, "She's something else, isn't she?"

"Yes," Joanna agreed, although she couldn't

think what. There was an aura about Rena, as if she were reflecting a golden sunset.

It was awhile before she noticed that Matt had changed his clothes. Instead of the T-shirt and corduroy shorts, he had on a yellow sports shirt and tan pants. "You changed!"

He laughed. "You noticed."

Had he changed so that she wouldn't look out of place? Maybe he was more thoughtful than she had imagined.

They did not discuss Rena during the dark drive to Santa Rosita Hills, yet the white room, the ocean's muffled roar, and Rena's serene smile stayed with Joanna. She was still thinking about her as they pulled up at the lighted gatehouse leading into Santa Rosita Hills.

"Evening, Matt," the elderly uniformed guard said. The light from the gatehouse slanted across his smiling face. He was clearly pleased to see Matt.

Matt grinned at him. "Hi, Hank. We're going to Melanie Tillinghast's party."

"Saw your name on the list," the guard said, pushing the button that opened the road gate. He glanced at Joanna and smiled his approval as he waved them on. "Have a good time."

Joanna caught her breath. It was the first time she had ever been in the gated community of Santa Rosita Hills.

She glanced around as their headlights pierced the darkness. On either side of the road there were orange groves; here and there white wooden fences lined riding trails. There were driveways with impressive entry posts and gates. In the distance towering eucalyptus trees swayed with the wind against the night sky.

Heidi lives here somewhere, she thought, watching for the Matthias name on the few entry gates that were lighted. She wondered if Heidi would be at

34

the party. After all, she had known Melanie for so long.

No, she decided. Heidi probably wouldn't come if she were invited. Heidi didn't seem to care about being popular at all. Strange . . .

"Here we are," Matt said, pulling into a driveway that curved gently uphill between rows of small subdued lights. Perhaps twenty parked cars lined both sides of the driveway. "Guess this is as close as we'll get," he said, parking the Corvette.

As they made their way up the driveway, Joanna could hardly believe the magnificent two-story Tudor house that sprawled across the top of the hill. In the glow of night lighting, the lawns and hedges looked perfectly manicured, as though a crew of gardeners groomed the estate daily.

"The party's back by the pool," Matt said, although anyone could hear the beat of rock music thumping out from behind the house. "Sounds like a great party. Melanie's mom and grandparents are out of town as usual."

Joanna wondered if that meant no adults. In Kansas parents usually hung around at teen parties.

As they stepped through the gate, Joanna saw the lighted Olympic-sized pool. A group of boys swung a bikini-clad girl by her arms and legs, back and forth, back and forth, until they let fly. She landed in the shimmering blue water with a splash amid the laughter.

Someone was bouncing on the diving board: Chad Chandler from her American lit. class. His jet black hair was wet and curling; his face split in a wide grin as if he were delighted to show off his athletic physique.

Joanna couldn't help noticing his muscular shoulders and arms as he dived in. "I didn't know we'd be swimming," she said to Matt. "I didn't bring a suit."

Matt darted a surprised glance at her. "There're

always extra suits for guests in the cabana dressing rooms."

"Oh," she said, "sure." She felt foolish, as if she should have somehow guessed that swimsuits would be provided for guests.

She looked at the white building on the near side of the pool. That had to be the cabana. There were doors all along it and, in front, a table presided over by a bartender in a white jacket. She hoped that she wasn't gaping, but it looked like a scene from a movie.

"Hello, hello, hello!" Matt shouted over the blaring music. He danced in crazily. "You didn't wait for us to begin."

"Man, we got started drinking out on the parking lot at noon," someone yelled.

"You started drinking in fifth grade," someone else said, starting a chorus of laughter.

Joanna smiled, feeling everyone's eyes turn to her. What were they thinking? Maybe Matt was making his big entrance, but the spotlight was on her.

She glanced at Matt and saw his look of approval. The Mexican dress was just the right thing to wear after all, no matter what anyone else wore. She could sense it. This was her entry into the popular group.

She quickly took in the setting. The huge Tudor house was at one end of the patio. The cabana lined the near side; on the other side there was a high wall covered with billowing purple bougainvillaea. The far end of the patio was open, giving them a view of shimmering city lights.

Melanie, with a swirl of her long purple cotton Mexican dress, appeared from one of the patio tables to greet them. "Hello, hello, hello, yourself," she said to Matt with a proprietary smile. She glanced at Joanna as if it were an afterthought. "Hi."

"Hi," Joanna answered, wondering why Melanie always averted her violet eyes.

Matt stood back, grinning. "For a girl whose name sounds like a melody, you're sure looking like a dirge."

"Same to you," Melanie answered with a tense smile.

He bent to whisper something into her ear, and shrugged. "I don't want to think about it tonight," she said. "Anyway, he'll be here. He's flying in for the party."

Who was flying in? Melanie's golf pro?

Melanie nodded toward the bar. "Go get yourselves a drink."

As they headed for the bar, Joanna asked him, "Who's going to be here?"

"Her boyfriend . . . friend, I mean."

Matt did not look happy about it, she thought.

She stopped in front of the bar and tried not to look surprised. There was bottle after bottle of gin, vodka, and bourbon as well as mixes, just as her parents had once served at parties. But here some of the kids were only fifteen!

Matt was looking at her. How dumb he must think she was.

"I don't touch the hard stuff," he was saying. "How about having some Italian white wine with me?"

She felt a sudden panic. She had never drunk anything alcoholic. It was bad enough with her father. Yet they would laugh if she asked for a Coke.

She could sense Matt and the bartender waiting for her answer. Well, she could pour it out when no one was looking. "Yes," she said, "some Italian white wine sounds lovely."

She accepted the glass of wine from the Mexican bartender, who was eyeing her quizzically. Perhaps she hadn't brought off her sophisticated act as well as she thought.

Matt had already sipped from his glass. "Hey,

Juan, just give us the rest of that bottle," he said. "I'll save you from drinking it."

Juan laughed heartily. "*¡Gracias!*" He picked up his own drink and toasted Matt with it.

Matt grabbed the bottle and led the way toward the patio table, moving with the beat of the music. "Looks like a good party, huh?"

"It looks great," she said. It really was like something from a glamorous TV show or movie. She could hardly believe she was here.

They sat down at a long wooden table with nine or ten others. "Hey, Matt," the guys said, welcoming him. They looked Joanna over almost as carefully as the girls did.

She could sense them slowly accepting her. After all, she was with Matt Thompson. That was the difference. Matt was soon entertaining them with a rendition of something wild that had happened last year at a party.

Joanna glanced around quickly. What could she do with her wine? There was no place to dump it. She thought that Matt had forgotten about her for a long time until he returned with the wine bottle. "Need a refill?"

She looked at her full wineglass, then smiled. "I forgot all about it."

He was waiting, wine bottle in hand, and several of the others were watching now, too.

She lifted her glass to him and sipped the white wine as if drinking were an everyday occurrence. It tasted surprisingly good. Not at all vinegary as she thought it would be. Looking over her glass at him as coolly as if she were in a commercial, she said, "So light and delightful."

They all laughed, and Matt refilled her glass.

Someone was passing a joint, but she waved it on smoothly when it came to her. She was surprised to see Matt pass it on without a drag. She hadn't known what to expect. Lots of the kids were smoking grass.

Later she wondered if it was all the wine or just being with Matt that made the party such fun. Girls and guys who had never said a word to her included her now. She had made it! She had made it with the popular group at last.

Someone turned up the stereo, and she was wildly dancing with Matt and nearly every other guy there, stopping only to gulp more wine.

Everyone was laughing as Matt and Chad grabbed her arms and legs and swung her threateningly over the pool.

"Let me get into a suit!" she protested, but she was already flying through the air, splashing into the bright blue water, embroidered Mexican dress and all. She struggled to the surface, her wet dress heavy in the water. At least the water was warm.

Darting them an indignant look, she swam slowly to the edge, pulling herself out. "I'm going to get into a suit." She turned to ask Melanie's permission, but Melanie was not around. Strange . . . She hadn't seen Melanie since the beginning of the party.

"Just take off your dress," Chad yelled, laughing. "I'll help!"

"No!" She struggled, but four or five of them were pulling off her soggy dress. "Stop it! Stop it!" she shouted, but it was too late. She had nothing on but her wet underpants and bra.

Laughing, they grabbed her arms and legs again and swung her into the pool.

She came up gulping the warm water and saw them waiting for her. She swam rapidly to the other end of the pool. Maybe underwear wasn't much different from a bikini, she thought, but something seemed not quite right about it.

She climbed out of the pool and dashed for the

dressing rooms in the cabana. Finding an open door, she rushed in and locked the door behind her. She stood there, hearing the boys' voices. It sounded as if they had given up. But what could she do now?

She opened cabinets and found a drawer full of two-piece bathing suits. A yellow string bikini looked as if it might fit. She slipped it on and looked in the mirror, amazed. She had never worn such a daring suit, but she looked good in it. Perhaps Matt would pay more attention to her.

Someone banged on the door. "Come on!" he yelled. "Let's see our new chick!"

She unlocked the door and, taking a deep breath, stepped out into a chorus of whistles and suggestive remarks. Where was Matt?

"If you're looking for Matt," Chad Chandler said, "he's probably off with Melanie. Old friends, you know."

Joanna swallowed hard and tried to smile as though she didn't care. "Come on," she said. "I'd like another drink."

Chad put an arm around her. "You look a lot better than Melanie ever did in those suits. I didn't realize you were so stacked."

"Never mind!" she snapped, wishing he wouldn't look at her like that. She turned away from him and hurried to the bar.

The evening became a golden haze of drinking, dancing in the starlight to rock, and occasional dips in the pool. She vaguely wondered where Matt was, then decided he was rotten for leaving her. She noticed couples disappearing into the darkness beyond the pool, some with a bottle, others with cigarettes—of all kinds.

A bitter pang caught in her throat. What if Matt were out there with Melanie? No! She couldn't bear to think about it!

"Come on, baby," Chad was saying as they danced. "Let's go for a little walk." He was slowly easing her away from the lights, across the grass, into the darkness. "Come on," he said urgently. He grabbed for her roughly, and she slid just out of his grasp and dashed away.

She ran wildly, but he was closing in on her despite the darkness. Then he cursed, tripping over a flower bed. He fell with a thud.

Frantic, she ran for an open sliding glass door in the house. A bedroom! A light glowed from the adjoining bathroom. She crept into the bedroom quietly and slid the door shut behind her. She locked it and caught a deep breath. She was safe!

Glancing around, she found a dark corner of the room and went to sit down on the carpeting, exhausted. She would let Chad cool off before she went out there again.

After a while she crawled toward a small window above a built-in desk. There was just enough light coming in to see the books on the desk. Melanie's school books! It was Melanie's room.

Joanna stood up to look out the window. From this distance the party looked different from when she had been in the middle of it. A few couples danced wildly to the music blaring out into the night; others were in the pool; some sat around tables. Someone was heading across the lawn for the pool. Chad! He rushed to the edge and dived in.

Relieved, she stepped forward, tipping something over. She waited, paralyzed, wondering if anyone had heard.

No one came.

Reaching down, she found Melanie's wastebasket on its side, papers spilling out across the carpeting. She brushed the papers together and put everything back into the wastebasket. She ran her hand across the carpeting again to see if she had missed anything. Her fingers touched a scrap of crumpled paper.

A voice in the hallway startled her. Melanie? It sounded like her!

Joanna grabbed the paper, rushed to the sliding glass door, and let herself out into the darkness. She started toward the swimming pool.

Chad was swimming.

There was Matt! He was yelling out, "Everyone drink up! Last drink!"

Where had he been? He was obviously looking for her, then saw her coming out of the shadows. "Well, my lovely," he said, "one more drink." He grabbed her hand and led her to the bar.

He didn't seem drunk, she thought, although she was still floating. She noticed his pants legs. There were dry stickers clinging to them here and there. Had he been hiking over the countryside?

He was talking to the bartender, something about Melanie wanting him to close up the bar.

Where had he been with Melanie? she wondered, then was aware of the crumbled scrap of paper in her hand. After turning her back to them, she opened it and, in the dim light, read the wrinkled words "Sorry, darlings, I just don't want to go on . . ."

The rest of the words were torn away.

Joanna froze. What could it mean? Maybe it was only a composition for Melanie's English class . . . or something else logical. She crumpled it tightly in her fist. How could she explain taking a note from Melanie's wastebasket?

Matt handed her a glass of wine, and she gulped it. "Hasn't it been a great party?" she said, although the words came out like stones.

"Drink up," he called out to everyone.

She emptied her glass quickly, hoping it would

42

make her forget Matt's disappearing most of the evening and Chad's chasing her . . . and whatever it was that Melanie had written. Especially if it was what it first sounded like. If it was a suicide note.

CHAPTER 4

Joanna awakened to the faint smell of smoke the next morning. She sat up groggily, glancing around her bedroom. Everything seemed fine. In fact, everything looked almost perfect. She remembered straightening up the room yesterday afternoon.

As she sat up, her head throbbed dully. Could it be a hangover? Of course not.

She got up and headed for the bathroom medicine cabinet and took two aspirin. Her Mexican dress, hanging on the shower bar, was almost dry now, and she vaguely recalled the guys' pulling it off. No! She didn't want to remember.

The smell of smoke was stronger. After hurrying to her bedroom window, she held the leafy green and white draperies open. The sky was tinged a garish pink. Fire! Somewhere beyond the dry hillsides near them there was a big fire.

"Joanna?" Cathy whispered, knocking softly on the door.

"Just a minute." Joanna pulled her pink robe on over her pink cotton nightgown. "Come on in, Cathy."

"Did I wake you up?" Cathy asked, bouncing into the room in her pajamas. "I want to hear all about your date with Matt. He's so handsome."

"When we find out where the fire is," Joanna said. She did not want to think about Matt—or Melanie's note. Noticing a flicker of fear in Cathy's eyes, she was sorry to have frightened her about the fire.

Their parents were already in the family room in front of the TV, watching the fire report.

"It's way up in the foothills," her father said, intent on the television pictures of the fire. He looked fine, as though nothing unusual had happened yesterday afternoon—except for his bloodshot eyes and the puffiness under them.

It occurred to Joanna that he always looked as if he were in control of everything. Maybe the doctors were wrong about his being an alcoholic. Alcoholics were weakling types, street bums.

"They have airplanes dropping chemicals on the fire," her mother said. "It's supposed to be out soon." She shook her head. "I can't believe that people would actually set an enormous fire like this on purpose."

"Crazy fools," her father said.

Her mother nodded. Had she already forgotten about yesterday afternoon?

She glanced at her father. He seemed to be a different person today. It was almost as if he had two personalities—one good, one terrible. Was that possible?

At breakfast Cathy wanted to know all about Matt Thompson. "Did he try to kiss you?" she asked.

"Oh, Cathy!" Joanna protested, blushing. Little sisters could be so exasperating. The worst part of it was that Matt had not tried to kiss her at all.

"Well, did he?" Cathy asked.

"Never mind, Cathy," her mother said. "You won't want us asking questions like that when you're older."

Joanna glanced at her mother gratefully, then noticed her father's angry stare.

"I should hope that my daughter isn't kissing boys," he said. "I expect you girls to be dignified."

Of all the nerve, Joanna thought. What right did he have to say that after yesterday?

"Just to quiet everyone's curiosity," she found herself saying, "I was not kissed, and I did not kiss anyone!" She stood up quickly from the table to walk out of the room.

"Come on, honey," her mother said. "We don't mean anything by it. It's just that we love you. Let's drop it."

Joanna sat down. She tried to eat the sausages and scrambled eggs, but her stomach churned. Why did they have to ask if Matt kissed her when he hadn't even tried?

She thought about the scene at the door last night. He had walked her to the front door and waited while she unlocked it. When she turned with an expectant smile, he said, "See ya, my lovely." And he was back to his car in a flash.

For a moment she had stood staring in amazement as he rushed away. It was as though he had not wanted to get involved. She wondered if it had something to do with Melanie.

"Did you have a good time?" her mother was asking.

"Yes. Yes, thanks," Joanna answered automatically, although as she thought about their date, she wasn't sure. She had hardly seen Matt all evening. He hadn't seemed interested in her. He would probably never even ask for another date.

"Do you feel well, Joanna?" her mother asked. "You look pale."

"I'm fine," she said, forcing down a bite of sausage. It tasted awful. Her stomach lurched, and nausea rose to her throat. "I guess I don't feel so well after all," she said, excusing herself from the table and running for her room.

She lay down on her bed, wondering if she had the flu. Or maybe it was the smell of smoke from the fire. Whatever it was, she felt awful.

"Joanna! Telephone!"

She opened her eyes, realizing that she had gone to sleep again. It was ten o'clock.

"Coming, Mom." Maybe it was Matt, she thought. Maybe he hadn't gone sailing to Catalina after all!

She hurried out to the hall phone. "Hello."

"Hi, Joanna," the masculine voice said, and her heart leaped. "This is David. How are you doing?"

It was a moment before she recovered from her disappointment. If he noticed, it didn't seem to bother him. "Hope you can make it tonight," he was saying.

Oh, no, she thought. She had meant to make up an excuse to get out of his church party tonight.

"Can I pick you up at seven-fifteen?" he asked. "Everyone will be coming around seven-thirty. I should be back here then."

Why not go? It was better than sitting at home. Anyhow, Matt would probably never ask her out again. "Sure, David," she said, trying to sound pleased. "Seven-fifteen is fine."

"If you get bored this afternoon, maybe you could help me decorate for the party."

"Decorate?" she asked. Hadn't he said that they didn't get involved with Halloween?

"We're using the Alaska trip theme," he said. "We've got posters and that kind of stuff."

"Oh, well, sure. If I get my work done. I have to help clean house on Saturdays." She was embarrassed as soon as she said it. Almost everyone had at least a cleaning woman once a week. David's family had a Mexican maid. His mother had just become an attorney and said she would never clean house again.

David didn't seem to notice. "Okay. If you get your jobs done, come on over."

If only it were Matt, she thought as she hung up.

It was four o'clock before she finished her chores. Why not help David decorate for his party? It was

48

something to do. Cathy had just finished with her jobs, too, and was ready to go to Dede's house.

"You want a ride?" Joanna asked. "Maybe Mom will let me use her car for a while."

"Wow! Okay!" Cathy said. "But I always walk."

"I just thought it might be fun to drive today. I'm going to help David decorate for his party tonight. I could walk up the hill to his house, too, just as easily."

"Driving would be wonderful," Cathy said, her eyes glowing with admiration.

It was difficult to be as admirable as a little sister saw you, Joanna thought.

As they stepped into the kitchen, her mother gasped. She was standing on the white counter and grabbed an open cabinet door for balance. "You scared me! I'm just cleaning a little."

Why would she be cleaning up there? Joanna wondered. The top cabinet shelves were full of punch cups, extra coffeepots, Christmas cookie tins—things they rarely used. She peered around her mother and saw the long necks of liquor bottles. She had taken the liquor from the built-in bar and hidden it up there!

Joanna pretended not to notice. She glanced at Cathy. She didn't seem to have noticed. "Can I take your car to David's for an hour? I could drive Cathy to Dede's, too."

"Sure." Her mother tried to act calm as she closed the cabinet doors and climbed down from the counter. "Just be home by five. I'll get dinner started early. Have fun!"

Joanna wasn't at all sure that it would be fun, but it would be better than staying home.

The hot Santa Ana wind was still blowing as she rang David's doorbell. She stood at the Porters' carved Spanish door, glancing around. Just below, she saw their new swimming pool. David said they kept it heated all year with solar panels. Far below, she could see the swaying eucalyptus trees near her own house.

A sliding glass door opened on the lower level, near the swimming pool. David stepped out, smiling. "Down here, Joanna. We're having the party in the rumpus room."

She almost laughed. A church party in a rumpus room! In Kansas, when people mentioned *raising a rumpus,* they meant a real uproar, really wild. She couldn't imagine that kind of church party. It would probably be calm compared to Melanie's party. She wondered if they would swim in the pool here.

"I'm glad you came," David said. "Just when I need help, too." He showed her in through the sliding glass door.

She looked around at the brightly decorated room. There were orange and yellow beanbag chairs, a well-used vinyl couch, and a big orange shaggy rug in the middle of the room. Bouquets of enormous, brightly colored paper flowers like the ones she'd seen in Mexico gave the room a festive air. On the long side wall there were posters of Alaska.

"Looks like a mix of Alaska and Mexico, doesn't it?" David asked. "Anyhow, it's cheerful. The Mexican flowers are from one of my parents' parties."

"It looks great," she said. It did. "How can I help? Everything looks ready."

"Over here." He led her to the back wall. "I found this Alaska mural being cleared out at a wallpaper shop. It's a little beat-up, but . . ."

Joanna helped him unroll the enormous mural. It was an Alaskan scene of green tree-covered islands in a bright blue waterway. There was a background of snowcapped mountains and a great white glacier. "It's beautiful," she said.

"It's the Inland Passage where we were. I figured

it'd cover a lot of the back wall, and when everyone walked in, it'd be just like walking into Alaska."

"It must have cost a fortune," she said.

"No. The shop owner gave it to me. He's a Christian."

"Gave it to you? He just gave it to you?" she asked. Even though it was frayed around the edges, a mural that big was expensive. No one ever gave *her* things like that!

"I've got these long strips of wood to frame it onto the wall," he said, then explained how he wanted to put the mural up.

When they had fastened it to the wall, they stood back to admire their work. It did make the room seem as though they had stepped into Alaska, Joanna decided.

"Won't your mother be upset about putting nail holes in the wall?"

David smiled. "I know it sounds crazy, but I sort of own the downstairs of the house."

"You own it?"

"Well, my grandfather paid for half of the house, and he willed it to me. He always used to joke that he owned the downstairs. See, he lived here before he died, and he had his room downstairs. The maid uses his bedroom now back there." He nodded to the other side door.

"You mean, he died since you've lived here?" Joanna asked. David's house couldn't be more than two years old. All the houses in the development were fairly new.

"Yeah. Last year," David said.

"I'm sorry, David. I shouldn't have asked."

"Oh, no, it's okay. He's in heaven. I'm one hundred percent sure. He was a minister, you know."

No wonder David was so religious.

He grinned. "Actually a wonderful thing happened when he died. He was right in that room down the hall, and we had a full-time nurse. He'd been in a coma for a month. Well, I used to come in and just sit with him after school. Have you ever known anyone in a coma?"

"No," she said, wondering what could have been so wonderful about dying. The whole thing sounded gruesome to her.

"They don't talk or open their eyes or anything. Well, you probably knew that. Except on Gramps's last day. He was just lying there quietly as usual. He had beautiful white, wavy hair; he was very distinguished-looking."

David was quiet for a moment, remembering. "I was sitting next to him on a chair, and all of a sudden he smiled! He really smiled and opened his eyes." David looked full of wonder, as if it were happening again right now.

"Then he waved. He waved!" David still looked amazed. "I asked him who he was waving at, and he said, 'Don't you see them? Don't you see them?' He looked so happy! And then his head fell back on his pillow, and he was dead. But he was still smiling."

"You're kidding," she said, wondering whom David's grandfather might have waved to. Maybe old friends and family on the other side—if there was another side. She'd never thought much about it.

"It's the truth," David protested. "Have you ever been around dying people?"

Joanna shook her head. "No. I've never even been to a funeral. My grandparents were killed in a car accident when I was little, but my parents didn't want me to see them dead."

"That's too bad," David said. "I mean, about the accident. I'm glad I got to know Gramps. He's been the most important person in my life.

Joanna wondered if David might someday be a minister, too.

"I'll never forget him smiling like that and

waving," David said. "Never. That was when I—"
He glanced at her, suddenly self-conscious. "Now
how did I ever start talking about that? Come on,
let's go upstairs and get the chips and dips ready."

That was when David did what? she wondered.
She followed him up the stairs. He had probably
called his parents or the nurse. . . . They didn't discuss it further as they helped the Porters' maid with
the food.

That evening Joanna was waiting in jeans when
David came to pick her up. There had been no problem about what to wear.

"I didn't drive. I hope you don't mind walking," he
said. "We can enjoy the sunset better."

Well, David was different, she thought, glancing
up at the sky. It was a beautiful sunset, awesome in
a frightening way. The sun shining through clouds
of smoke turned the sky a bright pink and lavender.
Here and there were red streaks like tails on comets.

"I've never seen a sunset like that," she said.

"It's because of the fires," he explained. "Even
bad can come to good."

She looked at him, wondering. Most guys didn't
get so involved with sunsets. *Even bad can come to
good?*

They turned as they heard a car behind them. It
pulled up next to them, and she vaguely recognized
two of the five kids in it from school. "Want a ride to
your own party, David?" the driver asked.

"Sure." David started to climb in. He looked embarrassed when he realized that Joanna would have
to sit on his lap. "Maybe you'd rather sit in front."

The girl in the front seat opened her door, and
Joanna squeezed in. David was introducing all of
them, and she tried to be very polite. But she wished
that she were with Matt, not here.

As they pulled up at David's house, two more cars
joined them. Everyone piled out of the cars and

headed for the rumpus room. She noticed that most of them wore Alaska T-shirts.

Weren't David's parents going to be here either? Didn't California parents ever stay home when there were teen parties?

"Wow, look at Alaska!" one of the boys exclaimed. "Where did you get that poster?"

David explained about the Christian shop owner giving it to them, and they didn't seem surprised at all.

Another carload of kids pulled up outside. "Hey, there's Gary," someone said.

Joanna looked over at the man with the dark curly hair. He was probably about thirty. He did a double take at the big Alaska mural on the far wall. "Where did you get that? It's fantastic!"

David explained about the wallpaper shop owner's donating it.

"Fantastic!" Gary said. Then he was greeting everyone as if they all were old friends, making his way across the room until he was in front of her.

"I'm Gary," he said, "the assistant minister at our church."

Joanna suddenly felt very formal. "How do you do." She wasn't certain if she should offer to shake hands. She had never met a minister. More than anything else she felt like making a fast escape.

"Glad to meet you, Joanna," he said with a big grin.

He did look glad to meet her, she thought. He looked like one of the kids, wearing a bright yellow Alaska T-shirt.

"Too bad you didn't go with us last summer," he added. "We had a great time. But you'll get to see it on film." He talked for a moment longer, then excused himself to get the projector.

Three of the girls had brought scrapbooks full of their snapshots and souvenirs, and Joanna found herself looking at them. Although she felt like an outsider, she couldn't help overhearing. It sounded as if they had had a lot of fun. Last year, besides Alaska, they'd gone to Disneyland and Magic Mountain in Los Angeles.

She glanced around. There was something very different about these kids, but she couldn't decide what it was.

A little later Gary banged a spoon against the big punch bowl for silence. "Let's thank God for our blessings," he said with a smile. The room quieted, and he bowed his head.

Joanna saw David bow his head beside her, so she did, too.

"Heavenly Father," Gary said, "we thank you for bringing us together. We are grateful for the wondrous trip to Alaska, where squeezed in that little boat, we surely became Christian brothers and sisters. We thank you for this food here in David's house. And we thank you for every blessing you've given us. Help us always to reflect your love. We pray in Jesus' name. Amen."

"Amen!" some of them chorused. Joanna especially noticed David's firm "Amen." She suddenly wanted to get away. Maybe they would start a weird ceremony. She wished she hadn't come at all.

The party went on as if Gary's prayer had not even been an interruption. She was relieved when someone turned on the movie projector and someone else turned off the lights.

There were movies of their crazy excitement at the airport and on the plane. Then shots of landing in Juneau. "How surprising it was to see everything green," someone recalled. "I thought there would be lots of snow."

The movie showed them climbing a glacier, then singing at a nearby church. The trip went on. They were singing to Indians in a dilapidated church, to loggers at a lumber camp, to old people in a retirement home, to patients in a hospital.

Joanna felt less and less a part of them as they sang along with themselves in the movie. "What a friend we have in Jesus," they sang. "All our sins and griefs to bear."

What sins could these kids have? It was stupid. They seemed too good to get into trouble. And why couldn't they bear their own griefs?

There were shots of great humpbacked whales breaching all the way out of the water, thousands of sea lions, glaciers, waterfalls, icebergs.

When the show was finally over, David said to her, "I hope we didn't bore you."

"Oh, no. It looked beautiful," she answered, even though the religious parts of the show turned her off.

"We're not sure yet, but maybe next summer we're going on a raft trip down the Colorado River."

"Who's not sure yet?" Gary asked from behind them. "Let's have a final vote on it tonight, and I'll get going on the arrangements." He turned to Joanna. "You're welcome to join us, of course."

"Oh, I couldn't do that," she said.

"Why not?" David asked.

She thought for a moment. It was because she wasn't one of them. And she didn't want to be one of them, no matter where they went!

"Anyhow, keep it in mind," David suggested.

"Thanks." She sat back quietly as they discussed the raft trip and voted, looking at each one of them carefully. Not one of them was popular at Santa Rosita High.

Someone began to sing softly. "Hallelujah, hallelujah." Others joined in until it sounded eerie. Soon they were all singing "Hallelujah" over and over. Some of them raised their hands as if to God while they sang.

Joanna felt more and more uneasy.

Then Gary was talking into the soft chorus. "I like to think about heaven," he said. "Not as an escape, but as the place that is truly our home. When we think about heaven, it brings us closer to Jesus here on earth."

Someone else spoke above the singing. "We're pilgrims on a journey to heaven."

"We are on earth only temporarily. Life is a spiritual journey to heaven."

Joanna glanced around quickly. If only she could get out of here without making a scene!

"Heavenly Father, we adore thee," a girl said in a hushed voice into the "hallelujahs."

Someone began to sing about power in the precious blood of the lamb.

They were crazy, Joanna thought, standing up to leave. She could dream up an excuse for getting out later!

The phone rang on the table next to her, and David grabbed it. He listened hard, his face turning white. "Gary!" He all but shoved the phone into the assistant minister's hand.

David turned to Joanna, stunned. "You'd better sit down," he whispered. "It's bad news. It's—there's been an accident."

"What is it?" she asked, perching on the edge of her chair.

"It's Melanie," he said. "I'm afraid that Melanie has—" His eyes widened with horror. "I'm afraid that Melanie has committed suicide."

CHAPTER 5

Gary hung up the phone, his face as ashen as Joanna felt. A stillness hung over the room as if everyone sensed that something was wrong.

"It's very bad news, gang," he said. "Very bad news. I can't even think of a gentle way to break it." He stopped, thoughtful for a few seconds. "That was the Tillinghasts' attorney. The fact is that Melanie Tillinghast is dead."

Eyes closed with shock. No one said a word.

Gary shook his head. "A maid found her in bed at noon today. Melanie took . . . an overdose of sleeping pills." He grabbed a deep breath. "Her family has asked me to officiate at the service Monday afternoon. They've asked me to invite all her friends and classmates."

Joanna felt cold. She had heard something about people who committed suicide—that they went straight to hell. If only she had told Matt about Melanie's note last night.

Everyone was getting up to join hands, to make a prayer circle. David held out his hand to her, and a girl reached out to her from the other side. There was nothing to do but join in the circle, to hold their warm, moist hands.

"Heavenly Father," Gary said, "you in your great wisdom know everything. It is not for us to judge Melanie. But, Father, we ask your forgiveness if we might have tried more to help her, if we might have tried harder to tell her about Jesus. We thank you that your love can conquer all things and that death is not final for those who love you."

There was silence. Then a girl added, "Father, forgive me for not trying harder to be Melanie's friend."

Beside Joanna, his hand warm in hers, David said, "Help us to know from now on when anyone is that desperate. Help us to be more sensitive to others."

The prayer continued, but Joanna could only think how foolish this was now. It was too late for prayers. Melanie was dead! They all should have done something long ago. She tried to forget about Melanie's suicide note, to focus instead on the words that the group prayed, but hot tears slipped from her eyes.

When the prayer was finally over, she turned away, fumbling in her pocket for a tissue. No tissue. Sobbing, she dashed for the bathroom.

Splashing cold water on her face, she finally stopped her tears. When she stepped back out, no one seemed to notice her. People were putting on their sweaters and jackets; some of them were carrying leftover food upstairs.

David came over to her. "We're going to church together tomorrow morning in remembrance of Melanie. Would you like to go along?"

"I don't know," Joanna said. Maybe it would be a good thing to do. After all, it was in memory of Melanie. But something in her mind said, Absolutely not! Don't go!

She glanced up at David.

"It won't hurt you to go," he said, smiling.

"I guess not," she said. "Okay, I'll go. But if you don't mind, I'd like to walk home alone now."

"Are you sure?"

She thought he looked a bit hurt, but she nodded.

"I guess I understand," he said, walking her out to the moonlit street. "At least it's bright out."

"Thank you for—" She couldn't very well thank him for a good time, but she saw that he understood. "It was fun till the phone call," she said. Maybe that wasn't quite true, she thought, but she didn't want to think about the party or Melanie or anything else.

"Yeah. I'll pick you up at nine-thirty tomorrow morning."

She nodded and started down the road.

A few minutes later a car full of kids from the party drove down the road toward her. She ducked behind bushes. She just did not want to ride with anyone or talk to anyone.

In the darkness she wondered if Melanie could see her walking down the road. Or was being dead like sleeping? Or, worst of all, was she burning in a lake of fire? A sudden vision of Melanie screaming from a pit of fire, red demons dancing around her, made Joanna run for her house. She had read about a fiery lake and demons somewhere.

She tried to wipe her mind clean of thoughts of Melanie and just concentrate on the stars glimmering in the sky—the Big Dipper, the Little Dipper, the North Star. If only she were still in Kansas, looking up at the night sky. She had been so much happier there.

As she stepped into her house, she was surprised to find a light on in the family room and her mother still up, reading a book.

"You're home early," she said as Joanna came in.

She didn't think that she should tell her mother about Melanie. It would only worry her. But to her amazement she found herself saying with horror, "Melanie Tillinghast committed suicide!"

Her mother's eyes filled with shock, and Joanna knew that she was probably wondering: Might her own daughters ever kill themselves?

"It stopped the party," Joanna said to divert her mother's thoughts. "They all prayed."

Her mother glanced as her sharply, then finally said, "That was nice."

"I said I'd go to church with them tomorrow morning—in honor of Melanie," she quickly added.

"I guess it can't hurt to go tomorrow," her mother said. "I just don't want you turning into a nun or . . . something."

What a strange thing to say, Joanna thought, although she understood. Her mother's teenage sister, Annie, had joined a religious group many years ago and refused to take her medicine for heart trouble. Annie had claimed that she was healed. But Annie had died.

"I wonder why Melanie would do such a thing," her mother said. "It sounded as if she had everything: money, modeling in L.A., a sports car, trips all over the world. You said she'd even lived in Europe."

Joanna nodded. "Something was bothering her," she said sadly. "Oh, Mom, why didn't I help her somehow?"

"But how could you know?"

Joanna told her about Melanie's party, about her disappearing and her family not being there. She almost told her about Melanie's note, but she couldn't. She just couldn't get it out.

"Where were Melanie's mother and grandparents?"

"Her mother was in Las Vegas, and her grandparents were at their home at Lake Arrowhead," she said, but she wanted to cry out, I was there! I should have helped!

"You mustn't blame yourself, Joanna," her mother said as if she had sensed Joanna's guilt. "How would you know?"

Joanna shrugged, dejected. "I'm going to bed," she said, and headed for her room.

At one o'clock she still hadn't gone to sleep. She

tossed from side to side, thinking about Melanie and glancing at the digital alarm clock. Two o'clock, three o'clock . . . She couldn't stop thinking that she should have told someone about Melanie's note.

At three-thirty she decided that she absolutely had to sleep. She had promised David to go to church for Melanie. After getting out of bed, she tiptoed to the kitchen and climbed quietly onto the kitchen counter. Opening the high cabinet where her mother had hidden the liquor, she found dozens of bottles of bourbon, gin, rum, vodka, and after-dinner liqueurs.

She recalled her father's laughing about cream sherry. "A lady's drink," he had said. "There's nothing to it."

She found a water glass and filled it half full of cream sherry. That much would surely make her sleep, she thought. She tasted it. How wonderfully sweet it was.

Having closed the kitchen cabinet quietly, she tiptoed back to bed with the sherry, trying not to feel guilty. It wasn't hard liquor like the kind her father drank, she told herself. Anyway, the important thing was that she could sleep.

The next morning she awakened groggy, vaguely aware that something horrible had happened. Slowly she recalled David's party, the phone call . . . Melanie's suicide!

She pulled herself out of bed, remembering that she had agreed to go to church this morning. She headed dully for the shower. At least that would wake her up, she thought, taking two aspirin for the headache lurking around her eyes. There was a bottle of antacid tablets in the medicine cabinet. Perhaps they would take away her queasiness.

By nine-thirty she was ready in her tan dress and new caramel-colored heels. As she stepped into the family room, she was glad that her father wasn't up yet. She did not want to explain about Melanie to him, too.

"Don't you want breakfast?" her mother asked from the kitchen. "Your stomach will rumble in church."

"I don't care," Joanna said, then smiled ruefully at herself. She did care. "I'll just have a piece of toast."

How pale and unhappy her mother looked. She was still wearing the old blue robe she had had on last night. "Are you sick, Mom?"

"I stayed up reading too late last night." She turned away to something over the range.

Her mother never stayed up late reading, Joanna thought. She was forever talking about keeping sensible hours. Was there something wrong with Dad again?

Cathy appeared in the kitchen behind them, rubbing her eyes sleepily. "Where are you going?" she asked, noticing Joanna's dress and heels.

"Church." Joanna bit into the hot buttery toast.

Cathy's eyes opened wide. "Why are you going to church?"

Joanna and her mother looked at each other. Her mother shrugged lightly as if to say, She's going to find out sooner or later.

"One of Joanna's classmates died," she said. "Melanie Tillinghast."

"You mean, she's dead?" Cathy asked. "Really dead?"

"Yes," Joanna answered. The truth of it hit her with a slap of finality. "Melanie's dead."

"Why?" Cathy asked. "What happened to her?"

Joanna closed her eyes. "Would you mind if I ate my toast outside?" She rushed out, not waiting for an answer. She didn't want to explain it.

Closing the front door behind her, she took a deep

breath of fresh air. It felt good to be outside. She glanced at the swaying eucalyptus trees, and it occurred to her that it had been Friday morning, only two days ago, that the Santa Ana winds had begun. Matt had stopped by to drive her to school. It seemed impossible that life could change so much in two days.

Thank goodness, Matt would be home this afternoon, she thought. Unless something awful happened to him, too. No! She must not think like that!

Concentrating on her piece of toast, she took a careful bite and forced herself to chew slowly. She must not, not, not think about terrible things.

She glanced up the hill. There was David's beat-up yellow car coming down the road. He had painted the car himself, and it looked like it, yet it was a comforting sight.

After pulling up, he leaned over to open the door for her. "Hi," he said with a sad smile. "I'm glad you're going to church with us this morning."

Joanna climbed in and slammed the door. "Thanks." She was still not sure that she wanted to go, but the car lurched forward. From everything she had heard about church people, they were a bunch of hypocrites. "Do your parents go to church?" she asked David.

"Not always," he said, sounding a little embarrassed. "They were at a late dinner party last night, and they're sleeping in this morning."

She glanced at him sharply, expecting him to defend his parents, but he didn't say anything. She stared straight out the windshield, thinking that if it weren't for Melanie, she wouldn't be going either.

"We're picking up Shirley and Stan," he said. "I hope you don't mind." He fiddled with his radio dial and found a religious station.

How could she mind? Joanna thought, trying to ignore the church music on the radio. What chance did she have to mind? She remembered Shirley and Stan from the party. Shirley had started the singing of "Hallelujah" as if she were already in heaven.

Joanna forced her attention to the eucalyptus trees reeling against the cloudless blue sky.

Shirley and Stan were waiting out in front of their house, smiling as David pulled up. How could they smile? Didn't they care at all about Melanie?

They climbed into the back of the car, talking as if not a thing were wrong. How could they call themselves Christians?

Joanna decided that she would be friendly but solemn in honor of Melanie. If they didn't like it, that was too bad. Yet all the way to church no one seemed to notice.

In the church parking lot a car full of kids was waiting for them. Another car with kids from David's party pulled up beside them.

Joanna nodded distantly. Somehow she would have to get through this morning, she thought as they headed for the large white church that looked like an old Spanish mission.

Church bells pealed out into the warm wind, and she followed the throng of people to the entrance. She hoped that none of Matt's friends would see her here with David.

A young minister in a long black robe turned to her. "Good morning, Joanna. Welcome."

She was taken aback momentarily, then realized it was Gary, the minister who had worn the Alaska T-shirt at David's party. "Good morning," she said, keeping her distance.

At the edge of the crowd a gray-haired minister in a voluminous black robe smiled a welcome. Joanna felt like running, but David's hand was at her elbow. He gently guided her to an elderly couple who greeted everyone at the door, then into the church and the swirl of organ music.

As she looked into the white sanctuary with its huge dark wooden beams, she panicked. She had never been in a church before except for two weddings. What if she was supposed to kneel or cross herself or something?

She glanced at David as they waited for an usher to come up the aisle to seat them. David smiled reassuringly, and she followed the usher up the middle aisle, wondering if everyone was looking at her. What if someone important recognized her!

Stopping near the front, the usher handed her a program. She took it warily. There was a picture of Jesus on the cover; surely that was supposed to be Jesus. She sat down between David and Stan on the cushioned pew.

Settling back, she glanced at the program again. The picture on the cover was like no picture she had ever seen of Jesus. He looked rough, like a thick-necked carpenter, not like the graceful statues at cemetery gates. His picture seemed alive in her hand. His eyes looked into hers.

She quickly opened the program. Perhaps if she studied it now, she thought, she wouldn't do anything foolish. She glanced at a quote: "Come unto me, all ye that are weary and heavy laden, and I will give you rest."

Well, she was not weary, nor was she heavy-laden, she decided, although it might be a nice thought for older people. And there were a lot of older people around her. They probably thought more about death than younger people did.

Hymnbook pages rustled as the organ began a new song. She had heard it before. David found the page and held the hymnbook out for her to share. There was a moment when everyone knew to stand up, and she was standing between David and Stan.

The music flowed through the church like a brilliant sunrise. "Morning has broken like the first morning . . . blackbird has spoken like the first bird . . ."

Yellow-robed choir members moved forward by twos down the main aisle; as they stepped slowly past the pews, their voices soared over the singing of the congregation.

David was singing out about rain's new fall and the first dewfall.

The gray-haired minister was now in the pulpit, and Joanna saw the enormous dark wooden cross on the white wall behind him. These people think that Jesus died for them, she thought. But why should he have died for me? I haven't done anything that wrong. I never asked anyone to die for me!

The minister read, "May Christ dwell in your hearts by faith."

Joanna mouthed the words on the program so she wouldn't look out of place. "That being rooted and grounded in love, we may have the power to comprehend with all saints, what is the breadth and length, and height, and depth, of the love of Christ."

It didn't make sense, she thought, listening to the minister go on about being filled with all the fullness of God. She gave it up. The prayer that followed seemed endless. Then they all were singing out "Joyful, joyful, we adore thee, God of glory, Lord of love . . ."

There was a Bible reading, something about Abraham, about Noah's building his ark by faith, about Enoch's being raised right up into heaven without dying.

It was crazy. These were all old stories. Even if they were true—and that was unbelievable—it was centuries and centuries ago. What could it have to do with people now?

She looked at David. How could he believe this? Had he and all these people been hypnotized?

There were announcements about a women's

luncheon, Bible study classes, a potluck dinner. Then there was more music, and ushers came down the aisles with collection plates.

Well, she was not going to give money for any of this. Anyway, she was David's guest.

She watched uneasily as the collection plates were passed, coming closer to her pew by pew. When a wooden plate started at their pew, it came to her with unexpected suddenness. Staring straight ahead, she took it and passed it on, barely suppressing a shudder.

A blond choir member stood under the great brown cross singing about her friend Jesus. Her friend! About how this friend knew her deepest needs and had walked this way before us. That every step He would lead.

Then they all stood and sang as the money was brought forward in the collection plates, "Praise God from whom all blessings flow . . ."

She understood now why her father said that churches wanted nothing but your money! And why her mother thought it was better not to get too involved!

She glanced at David singing out loudly about Father, Son, and Holy Ghost. She could imagine him wearing a minister's robe. She turned away. She would never get involved with anyone who was into religion again.

She thought about Matt, trying to imagine him on the sailboat, maybe leaving Catalina Island now, sailing home through the bright sunshine. How beautiful it would be out there. Would he ever invite her out sailing? She had taken sailing lessons one summer on a lake, but that was a long time ago. She'd probably remember what to do again, though, Oh, if only he'd ask her.

She looked up. The minister stood at the pulpit, preaching. He seemed to be looking right at her. She glanced away. He was talking about a great cloud of witnesses who had carried faith forward.

Finally they were singing the closing hymn. It went on about Jesus Christ and then a verse about the Prince of Darkness. The devil? Did these people believe that there really was a devil, too?

She glanced around during the minister's benediction. His right hand reached powerfully out above the people as he blessed them. Well, she did not want his blessing. She wanted to get out. She had come only because of Melanie, yet not one word had been said about her!

"Did you enjoy the service?" Stan asked as they stood up to leave.

"It was all right," she lied.

David, Shirley, and Stan made small talk and greeted people in the aisle as they filed out of the church.

Joanna turned to David. "Why didn't he even mention Melanie?"

He looked at her, perplexed. "No one in her family is a member of the church."

"But she's lived here forever. I thought that churches were supposed to be for the whole community."

"They are," he said, "but it's just like a—like a museum with a beautiful painting in it. If you don't go to the museum and reach out to the beauty of the painting, it doesn't do a thing for you."

She did not want to hear about museums and paintings. Melanie must have had some connection with the church. "Didn't her family ask Gary to speak at her funeral?"

David nodded. "I guess they didn't know who else to ask. Melanie went to a church summer camp with us once in the mountains, but none of them ever came to church."

70

Isn't God for everyone? she wanted to ask, but kept her mouth shut. It was the last straw when they walked out the door. There was no way to avoid shaking hands with the minister. "I hope we'll see you here again," he said.

"Thank you," she answered, but her mind said, Never! Absolutely never!

CHAPTER 6

Matt called at two o'clock that afternoon, his voice trembling. "Joanna, you've got to come over."

"Sure, Matt." She knew he had heard about Melanie. "I'll be there as soon as I can."

"Hurry. I'll be waiting."

He sounded upset. She rushed to her room for the denim handbag that matched her denim shorts and quickly brushed her hair, then hurried outside.

Her mother was sitting on the patio in the shade of the table's yellow umbrella. She looked up over the Sunday newspaper and noticed Joanna's handbag. "Where are you going?"

"Matt called. He's awfully upset about Melanie. Can I use your car to go there?"

Her mother frowned. "I don't think you should go. You'll look as if you're throwing yourself at him."

I don't care what it looks like, Joanna thought. "He called and invited me."

"Well, you can't use my car. Dad took it to the office." She looked down at the newspaper. "You'll have to use his car."

Strange that he was working on Sunday, Joanna thought, but there was no time for questions. "Thanks, Mom. Don't keep dinner for me. And don't worry."

Joanna remembered that Cathy was at Dede's house this afternoon. Her mother looked lonely.

"It'll be a quiet afternoon for you anyway, Mom," she said, impulsively kissing her forehead. "See you."

She swept through the house for the car keys and headed for the garage. She didn't like driving her father's new green Buick for fear of putting a scratch on it. She would just have to be careful.

Driving down the Coast Highway near downtown Santa Rosita, she thought she saw her mother's station wagon. It was parked on the block of sleazy bars. Glancing in her rearview mirror, she saw a man who looked a lot like her father staggering across the sidewalk. No . . . of course not. Her father wouldn't go to bars like that. Anyway, he was working at his office.

She tried to concentrate on how she could help Matt. Maybe, just maybe, he would get over loving Melanie someday.

As she pulled up in Matt's driveway, she remembered her first reaction to the house. Today again the modernistic house had a cool look about it, almost a chilling effect.

Matt walked right out to her car as if he had been watching for her. His hair was sun-bleached blonder than ever; his face, arms, and legs all the way to his cutoffs were bright red with sunburn. He looked miserable and not just because of his burn.

Climbing out of her car, she reached for his hand and held it for a moment. "I'm sorry about Melanie."

He closed his eyes. "Thanks."

She didn't know what to say into the uncomfortable silence. "I, well, I went to church this morning in memory of her."

He glanced at her strangely, almost as if he might cry.

Then she surely wouldn't know what to do, she thought.

74

"Thanks for coming," he said. "I didn't know who else to call."

Joanna nodded. "It's okay." Maybe she should try to change the subject. "You sure are sunburned."

He touched his red face gingerly. "Yeah. It was good sailing until we got the phone call at Catalina. We left right away this morning. So here I am now, and there's nothing I can do." His voice faltered. "I tried to help her. I honestly tried."

She remembered watching from the school bus Friday as he had talked so earnestly to Melanie in his car. Joanna had thought then that he was in love with her. Later, during her party, he had disappeared with her for a long time.

"You want to walk along the beach?" he asked. "I locked up the house."

"Sure." She felt uneasy, unsure of what might happen.

They headed out over the sandy hillside and down toward the ocean. There were few people out on the beach, considering how hot the wind was. Occasional gusts of wind lifted dry sand, whipping it through the air, stinging her legs.

She turned to him and saw his chin trembling. She quickly looked away at the bright blue Pacific.

Great waves gathered in the distance and roared in on the beach, crashing across the sand, foaming at their feet. They walked along the beach in silence for a long time. After a while the surging sound of the ocean made her feel calmer.

"It's good of you to come over," he finally said. "I don't know, I can't seem to talk to the guys about this . . . about Melanie. You know, I really—" He stopped, gulping.

I really *what?* Joanna wondered. Was he going to say that he had really loved Melanie?

"The guys would figure I got her pregnant," he

75

blurted. "That's what they thought last time. That's what her family thought at first, too."

Melanie had been pregnant! And people thought that Matt . . . Trying to hide her shock, she glanced away at the ocean. What did Matt mean, *"That's what they thought last time?"*

It took a while for her to get up her courage to ask him. "Was it the second time she was pregnant?"

"Yeah. It's the second time." He looked far away, up the coast. "She swore she'd never have another abortion. The first one almost drove her crazy. She had terrible nightmares."

Joanna was appalled. A few girls in her high school in Kansas had gotten pregnant. No one she had known very well. But twice! Melanie had been pregnant twice!

Matt's words were dull, as if something had gone dead in him. "She swore she'd never have another abortion; then she was going to have to . . . again."

"Oh, no."

"Oh, yeah," he said.

No wonder Melanie acted so cold, she thought.

"I drove her to a clinic for the first one last summer," Matt said. "Her family is always gone to Europe or Arrowhead or some stupid place."

Joanna had to know for certain; she had to ask. "Matt, were you—were you the father?"

"No!" His eyes darkened with despair. Then he was suddenly sobbing as he sank down onto the sand. "But I told her I'd marry her and she could get a divorce from me if that damn golf pro would marry her later."

"Marry her? But why would you marry her?" She had no more than asked when she knew the answer. Because Matt loved Melanie. No matter what else he might say, it was because he loved her.

His body shook as he sat there on the sand. "Because . . ." He could hardly force out the words. "Because I feel so guilty, so terribly guilty. When we were little, I . . . oh, damn, you know. I got her to play doctor."

He closed his eyes and grabbed a deep breath. "I went to her shrink once about that. He said lots of kids do it. Not to feel guilty. But I felt like I'd gotten her started, like I'd made her, you know, promiscuous."

Joanna couldn't believe this was happening. That, because they'd played doctor, Matt would offer to marry Melanie. That she had killed herself. "But why did she kill herself? Something could have been worked out. She might have gotten over him."

It was a long time before he answered. "That was only one part of it," he said, looking away. "The nightmares were driving her crazy. It got so she was afraid to sleep. She said she couldn't stand them anymore."

Joanna remembered the hint of dark shadows under Melanie's eyes. "What kinds of nightmares?"

"Babies. She dreamed about babies. They called her Mommy, and they reached out to her, first the one, and now this one, too. They would just be coming to her when a knife came from nowhere and lopped off their heads."

Joanna shuddered.

Matt looked at her, eyes wild with anguish. "The shrink said it was guilt." He made himself go on despite the tears rolling down his cheeks. "She just couldn't take it anymore. I should have guessed what she might do, but I didn't want to think about it, and I went sailing! Sailing!"

He was quiet for a moment, then added, "And Melanie was killing herself." Tears welled in his eyes and slid down his cheeks.

Joanna dug in her denim handbag for tissues and

handed one to him. She put her hand on his shoulder while he shook with silent sobs and was grateful that no one was near them, that it was November, not summer on the beach.

If only she had shown him the note, she thought. She wanted to tell him but she couldn't say it.

He finally stopped shaking and blew his nose. "I'm sorry, Joanna, I hardly even know you, but there's no one else I can talk to. There's no sense in talking to my father. And my mother is so busy with her new husband and their grand Palm Springs social life."

"It's okay, Matt. I'm glad that you thought of me." She wanted to put her arms around him, to protect him. No matter what had happened, she loved him.

He tried to smile at her but made a bad job of it. "I guess I was interested in you because you looked so sweet, so innocent. I needed that for a change."

"Oh, Matt!" she cried out as their eyes met, and she was in his arms.

He moaned with pain as their arms tightened around each other. "Please help me," he said, trembling, as they lay down in the sand. "Help me, Joanna, please!"

She kissed his forehead, wishing that he would kiss her lips. When he didn't, she patted his back gently in the warm sun, as if he were a small child. For a long time they just lay there together, holding each other until he stopped shaking.

At last he looked at her with a sad smile. "You really are my lovely," he said.

How lucky Melanie was to have had him propose, Joanna thought as they sat up and brushed the sand from their arms. She wondered if Melanie had even appreciated Matt's offer. What a terrible mess it all was. Yet she was glad that Matt had called her. She watched him reach into his pocket and pull out a pill bottle. "Matt?"

"It's okay," he said, showing her the label. "They're prescription pills."

She felt relieved. So many kids took drugs. "Are you sick?"

"They're for my back. I clobbered it playing ball last winter. Basketball. I guess you wouldn't know."

"I knew you were captain of the team last year."

"Yeah. Well, the doctor says I can't play anymore." He popped the two pills into his mouth and swallowed. "Man, when life starts to get rotten, it sure goes downhill all at once."

"What happened to your back?"

"I was going for a lay-up shot, and this clown from Puente High rammed me, just rammed me. They had to haul me off in an ambulance. Six hours later I came to in the hospital. I was all right except for my stupid back. The doctor says I'm stuck with it."

"I'm sorry, Matt. I'm really sorry."

He got up. "Yeah. Well, it hurts only when I overdo it. It was rough, sailing home this morning." He looked out at the ocean. "Let's forget it."

It did seem that everything in his life was going wrong, but she could make it up to him.

"Listen, I'm sorry for getting choked up on you," he said. "I hope you won't say anything."

"Oh, no, Matt! I'd never tell anyone!"

He put an arm around her shoulder as they started back. "You're okay, Joanna."

She smiled at him. "If only I could help you."

"You have. You already have by just listening."

There was something about his sad grin that made her feel as if she were melting. She wished that time would stop, right here on the beach, Matt holding his arm around her.

Later, as they walked to his house, she said, "There's only one thing that really bothers me, Matt. Friday night at her party you and Melanie disappeared for a long time. Well, then you came back with brambles on your pants. I didn't know what to think."

His face suddenly looked even redder. "I never even thought how that might look. I'm afraid it's a long story."

They wandered on for a while as he collected his thoughts. "You see, Melanie was expecting Russ—her fiancé, as she called him, although I don't think he ever planned to marry her. He had other girlfriends, too."

"Was he the father both times?"

"Yeah. Big-deal golf pro. He lived here for a few months. He was Melanie's mother's boyfriend."

"I heard about him," Joanna said.

"I guess it must sound crazy to you."

She nodded. "Like something out of a movie, the kind of thing I thought never really happened."

"Anyhow, Melanie and her mother didn't get along. I think her mother was jealous of Melanie being young. And Melanie stole Russ from her mother. Actually her mother probably never knew that until later. She left for France last summer, and that's when Melanie was pregnant."

"But twice . . . How could Melanie let it happen twice?"

Matt shook his head. "I told her to stay away from Russ after the first time, but she called him right away again. She could have had almost any guy in town, but she had to have the one who didn't really love her."

It was easy to imagine Melanie's wanting whoever was hardest to get. "But what about her grandparents? Didn't they try to stop her?"

"They tried, but once Melanie had her mind on something, nothing could stop her. She was modeling in L.A., and she moved in with him last June. She said she was on the pill, but she got pregnant anyhow. She hadn't told Russ this time. I was supposed to take her to the doctor for another abortion."

"That must have been awful for you!"

"Yeah." He kicked the sand. "It was awful all right. Worst of all, it didn't even stop Melanie. She would have moved right back to L.A. with him. In the meantime, though, another girl moved in with him when school started."

"How could she still love him?" she asked. "I just don't see how!"

"Beats me, too," he said, "except for that one thing. The harder he was to get, the more of a challenge it was for her. Maybe it's because all her life she had everything she wanted."

Joanna felt like crying for Melanie, for Matt, for the whole awful mess. "Didn't she tell her mother?"

"Yeah, she told her. She thought there might be a way to get him to marry her. But her mother just laughed. She said that Melanie was a damn fool, that Russ would never get married, that you had to understand men like him. Her mother thought it was an amusing lesson for Melanie."

Matt took a deep breath. "Melanie said she'd prove that Russ loved her. She said he would marry her. And she was so sure that she had talked him into coming for her party. She was going to prove to her mother and me and everyone else how much he loved her. Well, he didn't come."

No wonder Melanie had been so cold to her. She was losing hope, and she was already drafting a suicide note.

Matt glanced away, embarrassed. "I can imagine what you thought when Melanie and I disappeared at her party. But she was crying and wild and took off down the hillside. I tried to catch her before she threw herself down a bank or something else crazy. I finally got her calmed down. She said I should close up the party and she'd go to bed."

"So that's when you came back and told everyone to have the last drink?"

He nodded. "That was the end of the party. In more ways than one."

Matt seemed unaware that they were holding hands. She wondered if he'd forgotten their holding each other on the beach, too.

As they climbed up the sandy bank to Matt's house, she wondered what would happen now. He had called her so he could unload his problems, and it appeared he had accomplished that.

"Listen, Joanna," he said, "I really want to make a clean break from the whole mess. That's why I picked you up for school Friday. And that's why I invited you to Melanie's party."

A clean break? What did he have in mind?

He put his arm around her shoulders, and her heart leaped with hope.

"I need another favor, too," he said.

"Sure." She would do anything for him.

"Well, I was wondering if you'd go to her funeral with me. I'd feel a lot better if you were along."

"To Melanie's funeral?"

"Yeah." He looked scared. "It's tomorrow afternoon."

"But I've never been to a funeral. I wouldn't know what to do or say."

"I have to go to it, Joanna." His eyes pleaded. "You only have to be there with me."

He looked so pale under his sunburn that she knew she would have to go; she couldn't let him go alone. "Okay," she finally said. She thought that if it weren't for his arm around her, she might still change her mind.

As they walked up through the sand to his driveway, a white Jaguar pulled up, a man and a redheaded young woman in it.

Matt removed his arm from around Joanna's shoulders. "It's my dad," he said.

"Is that his girl friend?" Joanna asked. The red-head was much younger than Matt's father, maybe just over twenty.

"One of them," Matt said unhappily.

Matt's father got out of the Jaguar. "Matt, what's with Melanie? There were rumors at the clubhouse."

Matt looked uncomfortable. "I'd better tell you alone," he said, nodding toward the redhead, who was letting herself out of the car. Both she and Matt's father had joints in their hands and looked slightly stoned.

Matt seemed embarrassed, and Joanna wondered if that was why he had passed up the pot at Melanie's party. Was it because his father was on it? It felt like a long time before Matt introduced them. Then there was a silence as they stood smiling at her.

"Guess I'd better be going home," she finally said. "It was nice meeting you," she said to Matt's father and his date.

His father nodded, his eyes glazed. "My pleasure entirely."

"Yeah," his date said. "Nice to meet ya."

"I'll walk you to your car," Matt said. He looked as if he did not much feel like telling his father about Melanie.

As she slid into the driver's seat of the Buick, Matt said, "The funeral's at one tomorrow afternoon."

She started the motor, wishing she hadn't agreed to go to the funeral with him. "Guess we'll have to take the afternoon off from school."

"You really are a friend," he said.

She forced a smile, hoping that he couldn't see her disappointment. If there was one thing she did not want to be to Matt, it was only "a friend."

83

CHAPTER 7

The next morning Heidi looked up anxiously from her school bus seat as Joanna joined her. "Did you hear about Melanie?" Heidi whispered. She looked upset. "We were gone for the weekend. I just found out."

Joanna nodded, already dreading the day. Everyone would be talking about Melanie. The funeral, this afternoon at one o'clock, seemed too soon; it seemed as if Melanie's family were trying to get it over with quickly.

She smoothed her navy blue dress under her. She had worn it so that she and Matt could leave for the funeral from school.

"You were at Melanie's party Friday night," Heidi said. "What happened?"

Joanna did not want to think about it. It only reminded her of Melanie's note. "It didn't happen until after the party," she finally said.

"Melanie was wild," Heidi said, "but I didn't expect that. Never."

Joanna noticed that the two sophomore girls sitting behind them were leaning forward, listening intently. She glanced away, but not quickly enough.

"Why did Melanie do it?" one of them asked. "I heard she was pregnant."

"No," Joanna lied. "No, she wasn't." It was none of their business, she thought.

"She must have been on drugs," the other girl said. "After all, she OD'd on sleeping pills."

Joanna shrugged and looked away.

Heidi waited until the sophomores had settled back into their seats. "I heard she was crazy about an older guy in L.A., but he wasn't quite as crazy about her." She thought for a moment. "Still, I couldn't see her copping out over that. Melanie was always so tough. I can't imagine anything making her do it."

Joanna wished that the day were over. Or that Matt hadn't told her about Melanie's nightmares. In her mind's eye Joanna saw little babies reaching out, then a knife. She shivered.

"Will you be going to the funeral?" Heidi asked.

Joanna nodded, looking blindly out the bus window.

"You could go with me and my family," Heidi offered. "My parents have known the Tillinghasts for years so they're going. My dad is her—the grandparents' doctor."

"Thanks, but I'm going with Matt."

Heidi looked at her in surprise. "Oh. Well, sure."

Miserable as the whole mess was, Joanna thought, there was a special ring to the words "I'm going with Matt." It made people stop and look at her with respect. She wondered what everyone would say about their being together at Melanie's funeral.

Later, as they were getting off the school bus, Joanna saw Matt waiting for her at the bus door. She almost tripped down the steps in nervousness.

He caught her arm and steadied her. "Clumsy," he said with a small grin that quickly faded back to sadness.

"You scared me with that bright red face," she said, although it was far from true. His sunburn of yesterday was already turning into a wonderful tan, and his sun-bleached hair shimmered in the morning sunshine. His sadness, she thought, made him even more endearing.

She recalled the warmth of his hand on her arm to steady her and wished that he would hold her hand now. After a moment she said, "You didn't wear your dark suit." He was wearing navy blue slacks and a short-sleeved white shirt, open at the collar. He'd said he would wear a dark suit to school.

He blinked in confusion. "Oh. Oh, yeah," he said.

Was he on those pain pills this morning? She decided not to ask, surrounded as they were with people getting off the yellow school buses. Everyone seemed to be looking at them.

As they started up the leaf-covered steps to the school, she wondered why he had met her at the school bus. Did he want somehow to separate himself from Melanie in people's minds? Did he want everyone to think that he had already been interested in Joanna Stevens?

Chad met them in front of the American lit. classroom, looking subdued. "You going to the funeral?" he asked Matt, his voice quiet, concerned. "There's a group of us going together."

Matt seemed to consider Chad's offer for a moment. "Thanks," he said, "but I'm taking Joanna."

"Yeah?" Chad looked surprised and gave her an appreciative glance. "Well, we might not actually make it there anyway. It's not our first choice."

"You damn well better go!" Matt said with vehemence, then turned abruptly to Joanna. "See you at twelve by the parking lot."

The classroom buzzed with talk about Melanie, and Mrs. Ekelman did not arrive until long after the bell. There had been a faculty meeting, she explained. She looked down at her desk for a long time, then finally up at them.

"I'm sorry to have to tell you that Melanie

Tillinghast died early Saturday morning. Those of you who go to the funeral this afternoon will be excused if you bring a note to the office."

The class was uncomfortably quiet.

"Now, if you will turn to page . . ."

Mrs. Ekelman looked pale, as if she were somehow at fault, too.

All morning Joanna noticed more and more people with an almost guilty look. Everyone seemed to know about Melanie. Even freshmen gathered in small groups that dispersed too quickly and quietly. Solemn twosomes and threesomes of teachers whispered to each other. It made Joanna's own guilt about the note only worse.

At noon Joanna rushed down to the parking lot. Matt was already waiting in his red Corvette, a faraway look on his face. "Have you been waiting long?" she asked.

He was startled. "Yeah. I mean, no." He leaned across the seat to open her door. "I couldn't make it through the last class, so I've been sitting out here."

Their eyes met for a moment, and his turned away first. "I felt like everyone was looking at me."

She patted his hand. "You're just imagining, Matt. Why should they be looking at you?"

"Yeah. Well, let's go. We have to stop at my house for my jacket. I don't know—I can't seem to keep my mind on track. I'm forgetting everything."

"I'll keep an eye on you, okay?" she said, and he gave her an appreciative look that made her feel weak all the way to her fingertips. She suddenly remembered their holding each other on the beach and could imagine his arms around her again.

"Okay, my lovely," he said. "You keep an eye on me."

She was glad when they pulled out of the parking lot and he turned on the radio. It felt wrong, so very wrong, to love Matt so much when Melanie was just barely dead.

"I couldn't get through this without you," he said. "I've only been to my grandparents' funerals."

"We'll get through it." Her voice was firm despite the sinking feeling below her ribs. She didn't know how *she* was going to make it through.

By the time they picked up Matt's jacket and drove over to the southern colonial-style funeral home it was twelve-thirty. The parking lot adjoining the funeral home was filling up rapidly with Melanie's family, neighbors, and friends. Matt looked solemn as he nodded and waved. He seemed to know almost everyone there, and Joanna saw them staring frankly at her.

Chad cruised past them with his van full of kids.

Matt was delaying, taking forever to close up the car, comb his hair, put on his jacket. "Well, we'd better go in," he finally said. He took out his pills.

She frowned as he put one into his mouth. "Is your back—"

"Headache," he said after he had swallowed the pill.

They started toward the funeral home reluctantly.

A somber man in a black suit met them at the front door. "Melanie Tillinghast?" he asked. When they nodded, he handed them white cards.

"In Memoriam," the cards said. "Melanie Anne Tillinghast."

"The Blue Room," the man said, motioning them to a door from which soft organ music swirled.

There were others signing the guest book ahead of them, and they followed them through the overpowering perfume of flowers.

Joanna caught her breath, trying not to gag on the sickly sweet smell. Should have eaten today, she thought. Moments later they stepped into the rear of the large Blue Room. It felt as if she were walking into another world; then it occurred to her that she was. She was walking into the realm of the dead.

Row upon row of folding chairs was filling with mourners. The front and side walls were lined with baskets and sprays of flowers.

Joanna's eyes traveled to the center front of the room, and she stopped. Melanie's casket.

She must have stood there staring for too long because Matt's hand was on her elbow. "You okay?" he whispered. "You look white."

She swallowed hard and nodded, starting forward with the line of people, then saw where they were heading. Each person walked to the front of the room, then slowly, one by one, stopped to look into the casket at Melanie.

Joanna glanced around quickly. There was no escape. She and Matt would have to go up to the casket, too. She saw Heidi seated with her parents and other kids from school sprinkled through the crowd.

Joanna kept her eyes on the flowers as they moved forward, hoping she wouldn't faint. "We should have sent flowers," she whispered to Matt, who looked just as paralyzed as she felt.

"Dad sent some. And the senior class sent a plant."

"Is your father coming?"

He shook his head, his face pale under the tan. "No way. He doesn't get involved."

"Are you okay?" she asked.

"I don't know," he said, "but I'm going to make it."

They were suddenly at the front of the line. It was her turn to walk to the casket. She felt chilled as she forced herself to step forward and stopped at the white satin-lined casket.

Melanie . . . Melanie wore a white dress, and her face was nearly as white as the dress. Her dark hair and lashes were the only color contrast in the casket.

She didn't look as if she were sleeping at all, Joanna thought. She looked empty, as if she were made of wax. The bottom half of the casket was closed, covered with a blanket of pink rosebuds. They had tried to make Melanie look sweet and innocent, a sleeping wax princess.

She felt Matt's arm at her elbow again, and she moved on past the casket and to the rows of chairs, softly gasping for breath. If only they could sit down. She saw empty chairs next to Heidi and concentrated hard on the chairs until she was finally there.

Heidi was patting her arm. "Are you all right, Joanna?"

She shook her head as if she were awakening from a bewildering dream. "I think so." She looked for Matt and finally saw him standing, shaking hands with people in the front row.

"Who's that?" She nodded at the slim, elegant woman in a powder blue dress talking to Matt. She seemed as lovely and calm as the soft music wafting through the pale blue room.

"Melanie's mother," Heidi said. "And those are her grandparents."

The elderly couple now shaking hands with Matt were as slim and elegant as Melanie's mother.

Joanna thought that someone in the family might be crying, but everyone seemed composed and dry-eyed.

"They're holding up very well," Heidi said. "At least that's what everyone is saying."

It sounded like a compliment, Joanna thought, but somehow, if she were dead in that white satin-lined casket, she hoped that someone would cry.

Matt headed down the aisle toward her now, his eyes wide, as though he were in shock. He sat down next to her stiffly. "They're going to have her cremated," he whispered, sounding as if he could hardly believe it. "They're going to burn her."

Joanna closed her eyes. She did not want to think about it. No. She would pretend that she had not heard him at all. She glanced sideways at him.

He was shaking with silent sobs, trying to open his white memorial card.

She turned away to keep from breaking down. Opening her memorial card, she stared at Melanie's birth and death dates. Below them, it said:

The Lord is my shepherd: I shall not want.

He maketh me to lie down in green pastures: he leadeth me beside the still waters.

He restoreth my soul: he leadeth me in the paths of righteousness for his name's sake.

Yea, though I walk through the valley of the shadow of death, I will fear no evil: for thou art with me: thy rod and thy staff they comfort me.

Thou preparest a table before me in the presence of mine enemies: thou anointest my head with oil: my cup runneth over.

Surely goodness and mercy shall follow me all the days of my life: And I will dwell in the house of the Lord for ever.

Psalm 23

It didn't make sense. No matter how beautiful it sounded, how could it apply to Melanie? She had walked in that shadow of death and swallowed a bottleful of sleeping pills. God had *not* helped her. And surely she would *not* dwell in the house of the Lord forever. If there was any life after death, her soul was probably on fire!

She quickly closed the memorial card.

The murmur of the crowd grew, almost drowning

out the soft organ music. Old friends greeted each other. A short line of mourners had formed to speak to Melanie's family. David and some of his friends filed by the casket.

Chad and eight or nine others from school came in and sat down two rows behind them without passing the casket. Joanna wished that she hadn't either. Funerals were barbaric—ancient rites that belonged only in history books.

It seemed hours before Gary, the young minister, stepped forward to the lectern microphone. "We are gathered here today . . ." he began, and the words whirled around Joanna without any meaning.

He said something about God's forgiving anything if we come to Him, that we have love and forgiveness through His only begotten son, Jesus Christ, that God is love, and He forgives us for caving in to the pressures of this world.

She realized that heads were bowed in prayer.

"We trust her and her future into your hands," Gary prayed, "and we ask that we learn to be more sensitive, more caring to people all around us."

Joanna saw Melanie's crumpled note in her mind's eye again: "I just don't want to go on. . . ."

"Are you all right?" Heidi asked, helping Joanna up.

She saw that her row was standing, starting up to the casket. Now what? she wondered, glancing at Matt.

He was biting his lips hard, but tears streamed down his cheeks. He blotted them with his folded handkerchief. "I can't make it," he whispered. "I can't make it."

They were next to move forward.

"You have to," she whispered back, not knowing if she could herself. "Concentrate on the flowers."

He grabbed her elbow with a painful grip, and

they moved slowly forward until they were at the casket. She could not concentrate on the flowers. Her eyes moved to the white waxen princess, the shell of Melanie, and she knew she would never forget this day.

Matt shoved her elbow, and they were trying not to rush from the pale blue room too fast. They were in the pale blue vestibule, then at the pale blue front door . . .

Hot wind and sunshine washed over her, and she stood there for a moment, just breathing in the fresh air.

Slowly she became aware of the long black limousine waiting for Melanie's family.

Matt grabbed her hand. "Come on, I have to get away from here!"

"It's over, Matt," she said, pulling him back until he slowed to a fast walk. "People are looking at you. It's over."

His eyes were dry when they reached his car. "Not for me, it's not over!" He stared briefly at the black limousine behind them again. "It's never going to be over!"

He sounded wild. "You want me to drive?"

"No. I have to drive."

For a long time he just sat there in the car, not turning on the ignition. Just staring. He wasn't seeing anything in particular, she realized. His mind was flipping through the past, looking at memories of Melanie. "Come on, I'll drive, Matt!"

He shook his head as if he had realized where he was, then started the car. "We have to go to Melanie's house. Her mother is expecting all of us there."

"You're kidding!"

"No. It's customary," he said, his voice sounding numb. "They'll probably have a bar and ham and cheeses. All of that. Everybody does it, I guess."

"I can't believe that people would have a—a party."

"It's customary," he said again. "It's customary!"

Chad's van pulled out onto the street.

"Are Chad and the rest of them going?" she asked, numb.

"I guess so. They've all known her since we were kids, too," he said as they pulled out of the parking lot. They followed Chad's van onto the main road. "It's part of life," Matt said. "That's what my dad said anyhow. Part of life . . ."

Then why hadn't his father come to the funeral if it was part of life? Joanna wanted to ask. She turned on the radio to the rock station and tried to keep her mind on the music. At least music had a more predictable beat than life.

Pulling up to the gatehouse at Santa Rosita Hills, she recalled Friday night, when she had first come here. It had been night, but life had sparkled with bright excitement. Now the sun beamed over them, and life felt hideously dark.

The uniformed guard stepped forward, the same man as the other night. "Good afternoon, Matt."

Matt was unsmiling now. "Hi, Hank. We're going to the Tillinghast house."

"I was sorry to hear about it," Hank said, pushing the button that opened the road gate.

Matt nodded. "Thanks."

Inside the gate Joanna looked at the rolling hillsides of orange and lemon groves, the acres of white-fenced horse pastures. There were horseback riders on the trails, riding along in the hot wind as if nothing unpleasant had happened in the world. In the distance, large houses sprawled across hilltops.

It was unreal, she thought. As unreal as the last four days had been. When would life ever get back to normal? It seemed that everything had gone wrong

95

with the coming of the Santa Ana winds. She suddenly wondered if David and his church friends called them devil winds.

"You're quiet," Matt said.

"You too."

"Do you suppose we'll ever get over this?" he asked, his lips trembling.

"Maybe—maybe after a while," she said, not at all sure.

He pulled up into the Tillinghast driveway. "Melanie doesn't live here anymore," he said, his voice shaking. He steered the car into a narrow parking space between cars and turned off the ignition. Reaching into his suit pocket, he pulled out his pill vial.

"Is your back still hurting?" she asked, uneasy.

"Don't nag." He sat with a pill in his hand for a moment, then popped it into his mouth and swallowed hard. "Come on, let's go in. Let's get it over with."

She was glad that he grabbed her hand and held it tightly as they walked up the driveway. Even while they waited for Chad and the others to unload from their cars, Matt held onto her hand. He was holding it when they walked up to the house and through its wide-open double doors.

"The bar's outside," someone said.

They walked through the long Tudor living room with a stone fireplace that covered most of the far wall, then outside again through the open French doors. The patio, bright with flowers, had tables and chairs around the pool, just as it had been for Melanie's party. Her family was not in sight.

Matt held her hand all the way to the bar. "Double scotch," he said to Juan, then turned to Joanna, waiting for her order.

"Just white wine, I guess."

Matt took his drink and gulped it down. "Awful," he said to Juan with a grimace. "I'll have another one."

Joanna felt her stomach churn. Matt sounded almost like her father! She glanced at him standing next to her, blond hair glistening in the sunshine. No, he was nothing at all like her father. Matt was special, like no one she had ever known.

She and Matt were on their next drink when they sat down with Chad and the others.

"I got started on the booze right outside that funeral home," Chad said. "That's the only way I could get myself in there."

Time swirled around them like the sunshine. It seemed hours later when Melanie's grandparents stopped by to thank them for coming. "Now don't be shy about eating," Mr. Tillinghast said. "The food is in the dining room."

"We'd better eat something," Chad said. "I'm barely standing."

It looked as though Chad were afloat. His eyes seemed unfocused. She hoped that he didn't intend to chase her across the yard again as he had Friday night.

"Aren't you reeling yet?" he asked her. "You're sure putting that wine away."

"Let's have something to eat," she said to Matt, ignoring Chad. She led Matt to the dining room.

The long table was laden with mounds of sliced ham, turkey, roast beef, and cheeses; trays of breads and rolls; potato salad, coleslaw, crab salad. The buffet held rich cakes, pies, cookies, and boxes of expensive chocolates.

"I haven't eaten all day!" she said, just remembering.

"You have to be home for dinner?" Matt asked.

"I told Mom I'd probably be late. Maybe I'd better

97

call anyway." An uneasy thought skittered on the edge of her memory—something strange was going on at home. But what?

She glanced at the door into the kitchen. A woman was using the phone.

"I'll call later," she said, and followed Matt with her plate of food to the tables on the far side of the patio.

Chad and the others gathered around with their plates of food, and Juan brought over glasses and two bottles of Italian white wine.

Later Melanie's elegant mother stopped by. "It's so kind of all of you to come over," she said with a wan smile, then moved on, stopping to say a few gracious words to each group of people.

She was very lovely, Joanna thought. Melanie would have looked like her someday.

It was eleven o'clock before they realized how late it was for a school night. When Joanna stood up, she tottered. She looked at Matt. He staggered even more than she did.

He was laughing at himself as he staggered, then flopped down hard on a chair. "We really got bombed," he said, holding his head. "Well, it was in honor of Melanie . . . beautiful, beautiful Melanie." He was suddenly sobbing.

"Come on, Matt," Joanna said, trying to tug him to his feet, but she couldn't move him.

"Okay, Matt," Chad said, grabbing him under an arm. "Looks like this time I drive you home. You can leave your wheels here."

Joanna lifted Matt's other arm over her shoulder, and they began to stagger out together with him.

"Bye! Thanks!" Chad yelled for all of them as they started for the darkness around the side yard.

"Afraid we're not making such a good impression on our elders," one of the girls said.

"Most of them are stoned or drunk themselves," someone muttered.

They glanced at the adults, who were staring at them with disapproval.

"We did it for Melanie!" Matt shouted back at them so loudly that everyone turned. "And don't any of you ever forget her!"

Everyone was suddenly quiet, looking at Matt. The silence held all the way down the driveway except for Matt's yelling, ". . . did it for Melanie . . . for Melanie!"

Joanna felt a terrible ache in her heart. Would Matt ever forget about Melanie?

"It's getting cold," someone said, and Joanna realized that the Santa Ana winds, the devil winds, had finally stopped. She wondered if their troubles were finally over.

CHAPTER 8

As Chad drove his van up her driveway, Joanna saw that her mother had left the outdoor lights on. The kids in the van were singing a raucous song at the top of their voices.

"Quiet, please be quiet!" Joanna pleaded, but everyone became only crazier. Matt was singing as loudly as the others, although he hardly seemed to know the words. "Please, Matt," she said, "I'll get in trouble."

Matt tried to stand up as the van stopped. "Wake up, neighborhood! Joanna's home!" he shouted drunkenly.

"Thanks. Thanks a lot," she said as she got out. She slid the van door shut quickly, grateful at least that its windows were closed as everyone shouted good night. She rushed to the house, thinking that she would have to act sober if her mother were up.

The front door opened, and Joanna caught her breath. Her mother stood at the door.

"Hi, Mom."

"Are you all right?" her mother asked, letting Joanna in. "It's so late for a Monday night. I thought you'd at least call." As she closed the door, her eyes widened. "Have you been drinking, Joanna?"

"Just some Italian wine at the Tillinghasts', Mom. Not much."

"Not much?" her mother echoed, following her through the entry. "You reek of it!"

Joanna stopped, frightened by the anger in her mother's voice.

"How could you do it! How could you!" Her mother's face was white. "I just got your drunken father home from the police station and put him to bed. And now you!"

"The police station!" Joanna's head cleared quickly. "What happened to Dad?"

"He's been drinking since Saturday night, that's what. He hasn't been home for two days." Her voice was full of anger, but tears burst from her eyes. "Here I am trying to protect you girls from reality, and you come home drunk!"

Joanna hugged her mother. "I'm sorry, Mom. I didn't know." As she backed away, she remembered. "I thought I saw Dad Sunday on the way to Matt's."

"Where?"

"By those awful bars on the Coast Highway."

"Why didn't you call me?" her mother asked.

Joanna shook her head. "I just didn't think it could be him."

"Well, it was," her mother said. "Now I have to sober him up for work tomorrow. He didn't make it to the office today, and I had to lie for him again."

"Is he okay now?"

"He's wretched. But he'll probably be all right in the morning."

"I'm sorry, Mom." She wished she could explain how sorry she was.

"I don't need another drunk in this family!"

"It was the funeral," Joanna protested. "It was hideous. Then the Tillinghasts insisted that we come over, and we didn't eat properly all day. All I drank was white wine. I'd never drink whiskey and gin . . . that hard stuff."

"Thank goodness for that," her mother said. She looked away for a moment. "I'm afraid that if this happens again, we're going to have to send your father to a hospital or a clinic."

"Oh, Mom," Joanna said in agony.

"Well, I have to get to bed. I'm exhausted." Her mother headed down the hallway.

"Good night, Mom. I love you."

Her mother turned with a weary smile. "Night, dear. I love you, too."

How could her father do this to them? Joanna wondered as she walked to her room. She hoped that Cathy would never find out. What if everyone in school found out that their father had been drunk at the Santa Rosita police station?

She quickly undressed for bed. She did not want to think about the day, but she could still see Melanie in her casket . . . Matt staggering down the driveway at the Tillinghasts' house . . . her mother so upset. . . .

Even in bed she could not stop the memories.

She was feeling nervous and jumpy. Recalling that her mother kept tranquilizers in a kitchen cabinet, Joanna crawled out of bed. She felt her way through the dark house. In the kitchen she turned on the light over the range, found the pill vials, and took two of the tiny tranquilizers.

Maybe, maybe she should take a bottle of sherry to her room, just in case she couldn't get to sleep with the tranquilizers. She climbed up onto the kitchen counter and looked through the liquor bottles. There were two full bottles of sherry.

After taking one of them out carefully, she carried it to her room and hid it in the back of her closet. That way she'd have it later if she couldn't get to sleep. She'd keep it there, just in case.

After slipping into her bed, she was suddenly exhausted and quickly drifted off to sleep.

* * *

The next day Matt did not arrive at school until noon. He looked terrible, Joanna thought as he came over to her locker, but then she didn't feel so good either. When she got up in the morning, she'd taken aspirin and antacid tablets and used eye drops for her bloodshot eyes.

Everyone at school seemed subdued. The only good thing all day was that Matt walked her to the rest of her classes and drove her home. The next morning his red Corvette was at her front door when she started out for the bus.

It became a wonderful life, Matt driving her to school and home, walking at her side between classes. Their names were being coupled everywhere: Matt and Joanna . . . Joanna and Matt. People looked at her with respect. Joanna Stevens had risen from nobody to Matt Thompson's girl!

At home, family life seemed better. Her father was quiet, bringing work home from his office and taking it to the den with him every evening. Her mother looked happier. And Cathy did not seem to know that anything had been wrong. She was more interested in finding out about her new idol, Matt.

"Did Matt kiss you yet?" Cathy asked the next Saturday afternoon as they cleaned house.

Joanna smiled and turned on the vacuum cleaner. Matt still had not tried to kiss her. Last night —Friday—a whole crowd of them had gone to a movie. Matt had put his arm around the back of her seat, barely touching her shoulder, and that was all.

Anyhow, it had been an odd evening. After the movie they all had a few drinks at the beach in Chad's van, then went home early. The boys were going sailing at six the next morning.

As she vacuumed the house, Joanna hoped that they would be in early from sailing. Matt had asked her to meet him at his house. She would much rather have him pick her up, but he had already looked impatient when she asked what they were going to do.

He did not like being pushed. He was used to having things his way.

That evening, as she pulled up in her mother's station wagon at Matt's house, Chad's van was just leaving. She was glad to see Chad wave and drive on.

Matt ambled to her car, sunburned again and grinning. "Thanks for driving," he said, opening the door for her. "I'm beat."

He did look tired.

"Would you mind just watching TV?" he asked, looking a little embarrassed.

"Of course not." The truth was that she didn't care what they did as long as they were together. She looked up at him, wishing he would kiss her now, right here on the driveway. She didn't care who saw them.

"I have to clean up. You want to wait inside? Rena's there . . . and Dad."

She did not feel like making polite conversation with anyone. "I'll take a walk on the beach, okay?"

"Sure. I'll hurry."

She smiled as he rushed for the house.

After pulling off her sneakers, she threw them into the station wagon, then headed slowly down the bank to the sandy beach.

The ocean was silvery blue, reflecting the clouds. It would be a beautiful sunset, she thought, hoping that Matt would be with her to enjoy it. She realized that she did not like being alone anymore. There were too many unpleasant thoughts to crowd in, too much that she didn't want to remember.

She stood for a long moment, feeling lost in the vastness of the surging ocean. Crashing waves drowned out the world as she walked down the hard wet sand, then stood waiting for water to lap at her feet. Suddenly foaming cold water rushed at her, swirling around her ankles, and she backed away quickly before the next wave raced across the sand at her.

Turning to walk along the shore, she wondered if she could walk to Alaska along the coast. There were rivers and cliffs, of course, but it didn't seem like it from here. Maybe someday she and Matt could just walk away, far away, along the ocean's edge. She smiled at herself. It was a crazy idea, like in old movies when someone walked into the sunset.

"Joanna!"

A blond woman, her hair encased in a filmy scarf, waved as she hurried to catch up with her.

Rena. It was Rena. How much younger she always looked as she came closer. It was her happy smile and her luminous eyes.

"I was hoping to talk to you. May I?"

"Sure," Joanna said. She waited until Rena joined in step with her across the sand. What could Rena want to talk about?

"Isn't it beautiful here?" Rena asked.

Joanna nodded. She had an idea that Rena wanted to talk about more than the scenery, though.

"I try to walk here every day, and still I'm overwhelmed by the beauty of the ocean and the sky," Rena said.

"It must be wonderful to live here, by the ocean."

"Sometimes," Rena answered. "But a lot of people don't really see the ocean, even when they live right next to it. Living here doesn't seem to make life free of problems."

There was a long silence, and Joanna wondered if Rena was going to mention something about Matt's drinking or taking too many pills. "Is something wrong?" she finally asked.

"Yes, something is very wrong. I'm hoping that you can help Matt. You see, he's in for some bad news."

Joanna bit her lip. Now what? Matt still hadn't recovered from Melanie's suicide!

"It's money problems," Rena said. His father has had financial reverses in his business. He's going to put the house up for sale. And the sailboat—"

"Oh, no."

"Matt's been through so much lately," Rena said, almost as if she had read Joanna's thoughts. "I try to talk to him, but he's only known me for a few months . . . and I'm only around part-time. He needs someone to understand him, to help him now." Her eyes pleaded. "You will help him, won't you?"

"I'll try," Joanna said. But how could she help Matt with this? She stopped and turned to go back to Matt's house.

"Thank you," Rena said. "I'll pray for you."

Pray for me! Why pray for me? What right did anyone have to pray for someone who didn't want it?

"God bless you, dear." Rena threw a little kiss and started off before Joanna could think what to say.

She felt helpless as she watched Rena continue down the beach. She meant well, but . . .

Joanna wished that she had not heard a word that Rena had said. Especially right here on the beach where Matt had been so upset about Melanie's suicide.

The sun slipped behind a cloud, and a sudden cold wind whipped across the ocean. Joanna shivered and started back, wondering what Matt would do now.

Nearing his house, she saw Matt's father leaving with a young woman in his white Jaguar.

Joanna wasn't sure whether they saw her or not. If they did, they purposely ignored her.

She walked up the sandy incline to the enclosed patio and unlatched the wooden gate. Inside, a wall of glass windows shielded her from the ocean wind. She sank down on a chaise longue.

A moment later she saw Matt heading out to look for her on the beach. "I'm in here, Matt!"

How glum he looked, she thought as he walked toward the enclosed patio. "The wind was getting too cold," she said as he let himself in the side gate.

He slammed the gate shut and threw himself down on a lounge.

"Is something wrong?" she ventured.

"Just about everything," he said.

She didn't know what to say. "Do you want to talk about it?"

His eyes avoided hers. "I don't even want to think about it!" It was a while before he continued. "This house is going up for sale."

Joanna tried to look surprised. "I'm sorry, Matt."

"Yeah, me too! First, we sell the house in Santa Rosita Hills, now this one, and he's talking about a small condo."

"Your father must feel terrible about it."

"Who knows?" he said. "All he seems to care about is young chicks." There was a long silence. Then he added, "Oh, hell! Let's go get a drink!"

As she followed him into the house, she expected him to say something about selling the sailboat. Maybe his father hadn't told him yet.

In the den Matt stopped in front of the bar. "Do you really like me, just me as a person?"

Couldn't he see that she loved him? "Yes, Matt. I like you a lot."

He looked at her for a long time, then leaned down and softly kissed her forehead.

She waited for his arms to close around her, for a real kiss, but he only held her lightly by the shoulders. He only liked her. He only liked her, and he still loved Melanie!

"Let's go out for pizza," he said. "We could go to Morelli's."

"Sounds great," she said. It sounded a lot better than starting to drink already with Matt so upset. She felt as if they might drown themselves with booze if they stayed.

All the way to Morelli's and during their pizza and salad dinner, Matt kept Joanna talking about her old life in Kansas, about cheerleading for games, about the crazy things she and her friends had done. She brought out shining memories as if they were thumbing through her photo album.

As they talked, light from the red candle on their table flickered across their faces. There was a glow all around them, across the red and white checkered tablecloth. She felt as if Matt were part of the glow when she made him laugh with her at her memories. Yet it felt, too, as if they were only acting, reliving the past, pretending to be happy.

". . . and Cappie," she was saying, "Cappie, my best friend since kindergarten . . ." Oh, how she missed Cappie and Sara and Dena and everyone else. She suddenly felt like crying.

There were others from Santa Rosita High in the dimly lit restaurant. How happy we must look to them, Joanna thought. She glanced around at people in the trellised room with its green plastic leaves and reddish grape clusters hanging everywhere.

Did others pretend to be happy to hide their hurts? Did everyone see through her smiles to her loneliness in this new school, and through Matt's grins to his terrible heartaches? Her throat tightened so that she could hardly breathe.

Matt looked at her strangely for a moment, then excused himself to go to the rest room.

Had he noticed that there was something wrong with her? Did he care?

Moments later David Porter was sliding into

Matt's chair. "How's everything going, Joanna?" he asked.

Where did he come from? she wondered, her hand trembling as she reached for her water glass. She nearly tipped it over, but David righted it just in time. She quickly hid her hand on her lap without taking a drink.

"Are you all right?" he asked.

"Of course. Why shouldn't I be?" she asked, but her words did not sound convincing, even to herself.

"You sure?" His eyes were soft with concern.

She nodded, hoping that she would not cry.

"Can I pick you up for church tomorrow morning?"

She nodded. Anything to keep from crying!

"I'll pick you up at nine-thirty," he said, getting up with a glance at the rest rooms. "See you then."

She managed a smile but didn't answer. She wasn't even sure what had happened and glanced around the restaurant to see if David was actually there. Maybe their conversation had been in her imagination, she thought until she saw him heading for a table near the window. There were some of the kids who had been at his party. She turned away quickly.

Why on earth had she agreed to go with him? The last time she went to church she had vowed never to go again!

"Something wrong?" Matt asked when he sat down across from her again.

"No. Not at all."

Later, as they left, he said, "Let's go home and watch TV. There won't be anyone home."

Joanna felt uneasy, not knowing what to expect. "Okay," she finally said. She could almost feel David looking at her as she left.

At Matt's house they settled down in the den in front of the big color TV. He sprawled out next to her on the brown leather couch with a glass of red wine. What he wanted to do was drink, she decided when he poured a third glass of wine.

"What's wrong, you too good to drink?" he asked her, pouring another glass of wine for himself.

"That's not it at all, Matt." She did not want to tell him about her father.

"You don't like me," Matt said.

"What are you talking about?"

"If you liked me," he said, "you'd drink with me." He grabbed her hand and kissed her fingers; then his kisses moved up her bare arm. Suddenly he pulled away and turned his back to her.

She wanted him to go on. She wanted to melt in his arms. She wanted him to kiss her forever. What had gone wrong?

"Okay," she finally said in desperation. "I'll have some wine." Maybe that would really make a difference to him.

An hour later she was in his arms, and his kisses thrilled her beyond her imaginings. She wanted to tell him how much she loved him, but he would have to tell her first. She would not give in on that, too!

By midnight they were drinking their second bottle of wine, but he still had not said he loved her. "I have to go home, Matt," she finally said. She stood up and tottered. "Oh, no! And I have to drive, too."

"Follow me, my lovely," he said, leading her to the kitchen. "Would you believe that I can make instant coffee? Clever, eh?"

She watched him as he got out a cup and the instant coffee. Lately, every time he tried to be funny, it seemed to be because he was hiding something. "What's wrong, Matt?" she asked.

He turned away. "Dad's put the sailboat up for sale!" he blurted. "It's been the only thing that makes me forget how rotten my life is now."

She reached her arms up to him. "I'll help you,

Matt. I'll make you forget everything, no matter what I have to do."

Matt caught her in his arms, and they stood there holding each other for a long time.

Driving home, she was remembering that moment when suddenly headlights pierced the blackness and beamed straight at her. Terrified, she whipped the station wagon to the right, barely missing the on-coming lights. The other car roared past her into the night, its horn blaring.

In horror, Joanna gripped the steering wheel with all of her strength as her car's right tires shimmied on the road's gravel shoulder. Finally she was able to slow the car. She pulled off the road and stopped on the gravel.

Shaking, she sat in the darkness, picturing those headlights coming straight at her again and again. How could she have strayed over the middle line like that? Things like that happened to other people!

She opened the front windows wide for fresh air and recalled her promise to Matt: "I'll make you forget everything, no matter what I have to do."

CHAPTER 9

When Joanna awakened the next morning, she felt awful. She remembered drinking the red wine at Matt's house, then the coffee so she could drive home. She saw the car's headlights piercing the night, coming at her. When she sat up quickly, her head lurched.

Maybe aspirin would help again. She padded barefooted across the white carpeting to the medicine cabinet in her bathroom, hazily recalling that she was supposed to go somewhere.

Church . . . She had told David she would go to church with him! She couldn't think why now. She could barely recall David's stopping at her table for a moment at Morelli's.

"Joanna?" Cathy whispered at the door. "Are you up?"

"Come on in. But I have to get dressed."

Cathy stepped in quietly, her eyes downcast.

"What's wrong?" Joanna asked.

"Everything, oh, everything." She grabbed a deep breath, as if she might cry. "Mom and Dad were fighting last night. Mom said she's going to leave if he doesn't stop drinking!"

"Oh, Cathy."

Cathy nodded, looking too wretched now for tears.

Reaching out for her, Joanna wondered if Cathy had cried herself tearless in bed last night. She held her in her arms until she seemed a little relaxed.

"Cathy, I promised David that I'd go to church with him this morning, but you could go, too. He wouldn't mind at all. We'd have to be ready at nine-thirty."

Cathy looked uncertain. "I'd better ask Mom, and she's not up yet. She's sleeping in the guest room."

"I'll be responsible. Let's just get dressed. You could wear your green velvet dress and your new black patent shoes."

Joanna wondered what her mother would say this time about her going to church . . . and taking Cathy! Yet when their mother got up, she seemed relieved that they were going out. "Have a nice time," she called after them as they left.

It was a strange thing to say when someone was going to church, Joanna thought.

David was pleased to see Cathy as she and Joanna climbed into his car. "Hey, I didn't even think about inviting you. I'm glad you're coming along." He looked as if he meant it. "You could come to church with us, or you could go to Sunday school."

"I guess I'd rather go with you," Cathy said shyly. "I've never been to a church."

David seemed surprised. "Well, then, I'm especially happy that you're going. You can go anytime with me, you know."

How pleased Cathy looked to be included, Joanna thought, feeling better about going to church. She should include Cathy in more things. Maybe they could do something together this afternoon since Matt was sailing.

There were too many good people that Joanna didn't have time for anymore. Heidi was always inviting her over to go horseback riding, telling her to bring Cathy along; she could call Heidi when they got home.

The church bells were pealing all around them as the three of them climbed out of David's yellow car.

"It sounds beautiful," Cathy whispered to David.

"I always think so, too," he answered.

Joanna straightened Cathy's collar. At least she could get her mind off her parents' fighting for a while.

Inside the church Cathy's awe grew. Her eyes widened with wonder as she walked down the aisle with Joanna and David amid the soft organ music. She sat down between them. "What if I don't know what to do?" she asked.

"Just watch David," Joanna whispered, remembering how uncertain she had felt the first time she had come.

Cathy nodded. She showed Joanna the front of the program. It was bright with autumn leaves, Indian corn, pumpkins, and apples. "The Lord is good to all. Psalm 145:9," it said.

Then they were standing and singing "Onward, Christian soldiers, marching as to war . . ." The yellow-robed choir members moved forward by twos down the middle aisle, singing out mightily as they filed past the pews.

How could Christians be soldiers? Joanna wondered. So much didn't make sense.

Cathy's brown eyes were bright with wonder as the service went on. "What a friend we have in Jesus," she sang along with a shy smile.

Joanna turned away.

Then the minister was praying. "We pray for the sick, the lonely, the confused, the hurting people of this world. We ask that they might know that Jesus loves them and wants to be their friend."

Joanna suddenly found herself praying. "Oh, God, if you exist, please help my sister, Cathy . . . and please help my mother and father . . . and me."

She felt Cathy touch her hand.

"Look, it's kids from my class at school," Cathy

whispered. "There's Dede! I didn't know she went to this church!"

White-robed children were grouping in front of the altar, then looked uneasily out at the congregation. A woman stepped forward to direct them, and they all smiled, as if on cue.

"Jesus loves the little children," they sang. "All the children of the world. Red and yellow, black and white, they are precious in His sight . . ."

When the song ended and the children filed out, Cathy whispered, "I loved that."

The minister was talking about grace, but Joanna couldn't quite understand. The program said, "For by grace are ye saved through faith, and that not of yourselves. It is the gift of God."

Grace, then, was God's love, she thought. God loved everyone. It didn't seem possible.

The service was coming to an end with "Amazing Grace." The minister had said it was written by a slave trader, a man who had bought and sold slaves.

She tried to understand: "I once was lost but now I'm found, Was blind but now I see. . . . How precious did that grace appear, The hour I first believed."

How had this man who was a slave trader come to believe in God? It was strange.

As they stood up to leave, Cathy said, "Thank you, David. I never thought church would be like that."

"Like what?" he asked.

"So wonderful," she said. "I thought it would be boring and dumb, not so . . . beautiful."

David looked pleased, and Cathy looked happy, almost as if she had forgotten what had happened last night.

When they drove home, the day seemed full of sunshine.

As they pulled up in their driveway, they heard a scream. Her mother! Joanna glanced at David.

116

He had heard, too. "You want me to come in?" he asked.

"No, it's just—" She couldn't think what to say, then remembered something about scream therapy—a show on TV. "It's my mother's scream therapy," she said. "You know, to get rid of stress. Thanks anyway, and thanks for taking us."

Cathy's face was ashen. "Thanks, David. I loved your church."

As they hurried in the front door, Joanna heard her parents in the family room.

"Damn you, give me those keys!" her father yelled, twisting her mother's arm, trying to get the car keys.

"The girls are here, can't you see that?" she said. Her lip was bleeding badly.

"Dad!" Joanna shouted angrily.

He glanced at her in disgust, and her mother tried to pull away. "You're going to kill yourself, driving in this condition."

He slapped her face hard and pushed her against the family room wall, but with one desperate push she broke his hold. She threw the keys to Joanna.

Her father swore, rushing at Joanna.

She held the keys behind her, so terrified she couldn't move.

"Give them to me!" he snarled. "Give me those keys!"

Could this be her father? she thought, appalled. He looked like a wild animal and . . . She hated him, she hated him!

He grabbed her roughly and tore the keys from her hands. "Damn you! Damn all of you! I'm getting out of here!"

"Look at you!" their mother screamed after him. "Drunk in front of your children!"

It was her own fault that he had the keys, Joanna thought. "Daddy, please don't drive—"

117

"Go to hell, Miss Churchgoer!" he snapped, rushing out. He flung the words behind him. "You have to drag your little sister to those hypocrites, too?"

There was a terrible silence as the three of them looked at one another and heard the car start up, then leave.

"I'm sorry, Mom," Joanna said. "I'm sorry about the keys. I couldn't help it." She wished that her mother would cry, she looked so miserable. Did she too hate Dad when he was like this?

Her mother found a tissue and blotted the blood on her lip. "I'm sorry that you girls had to see this. He needs help. He can't stop drinking by himself anymore."

Joanna recalled commercials on television about clinics for alcoholics. Was her father one of them, one of those people? "But everyone will find out."

Her mother looked resigned. "People are going to find out even more if he kills someone with the car."

Cathy sobbed. "He isn't like Daddy anymore."

Her mother hugged her. "He's not himself, he's really not himself when he drinks."

But who is he? Joanna wondered. He's like an animal. . . . No! She must not think of her own father like that!

Her mother gave Cathy a squeeze. "Why don't you girls go to a movie or something this afternoon to get your minds off this?"

She was right, Joanna thought. They had to get out. Especially Cathy. "Maybe we could go horseback riding at Heidi's. She's always inviting me."

"Sounds like a good idea," her mother said. "What do you think, Cathy?"

Cathy nodded, her usual enthusiasm gone.

Joanna started for the phone. "I'll call Heidi now."

That afternoon on the dusty riding trail Heidi led the way astride her black mare. Next came Cathy, her pigtails bobbing up and down as she bounced along on Heidi's old pony, Dolly. Joanna, on a big chestnut horse, felt better as they rode through the sunshine and eucalyptus trees.

Had Cathy forgotten what had happened after church? Joanna wondered. Probably not. Probably never. She hoped that Cathy wasn't beginning to hate their father, too.

The soft clip-clop of the horses' hooves and the trill of birds filled the sunny afternoon. The smell of horses hung pleasantly in the autumn air.

The trail widened, and Heidi reined in her horse, waiting for Cathy and Joanna. "I don't know who's enjoying this more, you or Dolly," she said to Cathy.

"Me, I think," Cathy said, rubbing Dolly's neck and managing a wan smile.

Joanna felt more and more secure with the warmth and sure strength of the big chestnut under her. It felt as if he were taking care of her, soothing her as they moved along the trail.

Rays of sunshine slanted through the eucalyptus trees. She suddenly remembered that her grandfather had called the sun's rays the fingers of God. It seemed appropriate here.

"You could come riding with me most Sundays," Heidi said as the three of them rode side by side. "Sometimes I'm lonely without sisters or brothers."

Even without sisters or brothers, Heidi seemed happy most of the time, Joanna thought. Heidi's parents, elderly and European, were different from most American parents, but they seemed kind and loving.

"Do you go to church on Sundays?" Joanna asked without thinking.

Heidi laughed. "No. Should I?"

Joanna felt her face getting red. "I don't know." She patted her horse's soft, warm neck. "I usually don't either, but we went with David Porter this morning."

"In my family," Heidi said with a rueful smile, "work is our god: medicine for my father; the chemistry lab for my mother. I don't know what they'd do if they broke their backs or something, if they had to give up working. It really is their lives."

In a way work was already Heidi's life, too, Joanna thought. Veterinary school was all that Heidi seemed to think about. "Did your father ever think about being a vet?" she asked. Heidi's father had had such love in his eyes for the horses when he helped them all saddle up.

"He says he still does when people are unpleasant," Heidi said. "Horses are usually nicer than people."

Maybe it was better to have horses as friends. Heidi seemed happier than most people who had humans for friends. But was Heidi facing reality?

Later Heidi's parents insisted that Joanna and Cathy stay for a simple supper of homemade soup and sandwiches. Despite her parents' Austrian accents and their different ways, Joanna didn't know when she had had a nicer Sunday afternoon in a long time.

As Joanna and Cathy drove home, they talked about Heidi and her family. "You know," Joanna said, "we can be different, too. Maybe if we just try hard enough, we can change things at home. We just have to try very hard."

"Let's do it," Cathy said. "Let's really try."

When they walked into the house, their mother was waiting uneasily. "We have to be quiet," she whispered. "There's a man from Dad's office in the den talking to him about AA—you know, Alcoholics Anonymous."

"How did that happen?" Joanna asked.

"He saw Dad out drinking on the beach. He talked him into coming home."

Cathy's face turned pale. "You mean Dad is an alcoholic?"

"Yes," their mother said firmly. "Yes, he's an alcoholic, and we have to face it."

Cathy turned to Joanna. "Do you think we can change that?" she asked hopelessly.

Joanna shook her head. She felt like crying, even more for Cathy and her mother than for herself. Most of all for her father. He looked so miserably unhappy when he was drunk.

"Maybe we should pray," Cathy said, tears rolling down her cheeks.

It certainly hadn't done any good so far, Joanna thought, but why not let Cathy have some hope? "Good idea," she said. What could Cathy's praying hurt anyhow?

CHAPTER 10

Glancing out the kitchen windows on Thanksgiving afternoon, Joanna was pleased that it was such a sunny day. She swirled whipped cream on top of the pumpkin pies, thinking she did have a lot to be thankful for, despite her problems.

She and Matt had dated steadily for almost a month now, and although he had not yet said that he loved her, he would. He would! Someday he'd be over loving Melanie.

She looked at her mother, who was leaning over the oven, basting the slowly browning turkey. She seemed nervous lately; she was always taking tranquilizers. She had just popped two of them a while ago.

Cathy, cutting carrot and celery sticks by the kitchen sink, was singing a Thanksgiving song she had learned at school. She seemed happier today than she had been for a while.

Outside their father swept the sidewalk and blacktop driveway in preparation for their guests. He was not drinking nowadays. His AA friend picked him up for meetings three or four nights a week.

Just three weeks ago her family had seemed to be coming apart. Who could have dreamed that they would be having Thanksgiving dinner at their house? Matt was coming. So were David and his parents and Dede with hers.

Cathy looked up from over the sink. "Dede could hardly believe that we'd invite their family. They were going to have a plain old dinner, just the three of them."

"Maybe we should do things like this more often," Joanna said. The smell of roasting turkey made the day feel the way Thanksgiving should, and it had been fun, too, for her and Cathy to get everything ready for the guests.

This morning they had decorated the front door with an Indian corn arrangement. In the dining room they used a gold tablecloth and orange napkins on the table. In its center they placed a rattan cornucopia overflowing with apples, pears, nuts, and bananas. It looked perfect.

Her mother pushed the basted turkey back into the oven. "I hope this dinner works out. After all, we hardly know any of our guests well."

Was she worried about Dad's drinking during dinner? "It'll be fine, Mom. If they don't like apple juice or milk, that's just too bad."

Her mother glanced at her sharply. "I don't know. I feel as if it's the calm before the storm."

Joanna could not understand. Why couldn't her mother be happy now that things were going well? She had become so negative.

Their guests were to arrive at three o'clock, but the doorbell rang at two-thirty. Joanna ran for the door, still in her old ragged jeans.

Matt stood there, grinning sheepishly, his hand holding something behind him. "I'm early."

She smiled. "You sure are. I'm going to put you to work."

He held out a big box of chocolates like a peace offering, and she couldn't help laughing. "It's for your mother."

She reached up to kiss his cheek. "You get out of working after all."

"I'd just as soon help. It's so quiet at home alone."
He smiled. "Wow, it sure smells good."

She was so glad that her mother had let her invite
him. He was lonely with his dad out of town and
Rena eating in Los Angeles with her family. "I
should have told you to be here to help at seven this
morning," she said teasingly.

"I'd have come!"

"You can help Dad watch the football game," she
said, taking him into the family room.

He and her father shook hands and made small
talk before settling down to watch the game. There
was a comfortable feeling in the room, she thought
as she hurried to her bedroom.

After a fast shower she slipped into a white blouse
and the green quilted hostess skirt her mother had
just finished sewing the night before. She had made
matching skirts for Cathy and herself, too—the first
time that all three of them had identical clothes.
What fun they'd had trying them on.

When Joanna stepped out of her bedroom, the
other guests were arriving at the front door.
Dede and Cathy were already admiring each other's
long skirts. Everyone was shaking hands, looking
pleased about Thanksgiving. Her mother was accepting a pot of yellow chrysanthemums from David's mother.

Then Joanna saw them—gift-wrapped bottles the
men handed to her father.

"White wine to go with the turkey," Dede's father
said.

David's father chuckled. "Same here. Not too
original."

Her father thanked them, smiling.

What if he can't handle this? she thought, not
knowing what to do. She couldn't just grab the wine
bottles from her father's hands. She caught her
mother's warning glance.

"Shall we refrigerate the wine until dinner?" her mother asked. "Perhaps Joanna can take them."

Her father handed the bottles to her, smiling easily, but avoiding her eyes.

The difficult moment was over, she thought as she hurried to the kitchen with the wine. But now they would have to offer the wine at dinner.

When she returned to the living room with raw vegetables and dips, everyone was having a fine time. The party was off to a good start.

Later, as they walked into the dining room, everyone admired the turkey and festive decorations.

Joanna and Matt served apple juice, milk, and wine as her father carved the turkey. She worried that his hand might shake the way it did sometimes lately, but everything went well. She did not ask her father what he wanted as she came to fill his goblet. She simply filled it with apple juice. Only David's and Dede's parents were drinking wine anyhow. Even Matt had decided on apple juice, probably to please her parents.

There was a moment of silence as everyone was finally served. "David," her mother said into the quiet, "would you like to say a prayer? David's grandfather was a minister, you know," she explained to Dede's parents.

David nodded and bowed his head. "Heavenly Father," he said, "we come before Thee this day full of thanksgiving for our friendships, for Thy love, which we reflect among each other."

He went on, but fortunately the prayer was short. Prayers seemed strange in their house anyhow, although Cathy went to Sunday school now with Dede.

Joanna glanced at Matt. Maybe he would think that they were religious.

He caught her look and smiled happily, as if he

hadn't given the idea a thought, as if he were having a wonderful time.

Their eyes held for a long moment, and she thought that he was beginning to love her in a new way. If only he would love her someday as much as she loved him. Nothing would make her more thankful than that.

CHAPTER 11

"Aren't we going to decorate for Christmas?" Rena asked Matt and Joanna the Saturday before Christmas vacation. They were sitting at the kitchen counter at his house, eating chips and one of Rena's health food dips. "It's so much fun to put up a tree," Rena added, looking hopeful.

Joanna smiled. Rena was always so enthusiastic about everything. Sometimes she seemed younger than they were, but she was surely over fifty.

Matt shrugged. "I don't feel much like decorating. No one's going to be around except us anyhow."

Joanna wished he would do something, anything. He was becoming more and more depressed all the time. She thought he would be over Melanie by now, but he was forever talking about her, blaming himself.

Basketball season was getting him down, too. Despite having been captain of last year's team, Matt refused even to go to games now. Instead, he took his back pain pills.

"The realtors said that Christmas decorations are good for showing the house," Rena said. "We could at least have a tree."

"Okay, okay." Matt looked angry. "But not one of those damn white flocked ones like Dad's decorator girl friend talked us into last year."

Joanna and Rena darted a glance at each other. Matt did not swear unless he was terribly upset.

"Anyhow," he continued, "Mom took all the Christmas ornaments. All we have are those gold balls from last year."

"Sounds like a department store tree," Joanna ventured.

"I've seen better in stores," Matt said.

She thought about her family's usual Christmas trees. They had faded ornaments that went all the way back to her grandparents' Christmas trees. Her mother had insisted that the ornaments be moved with them to California, no matter how much it cost. Decorating the tree was always one of the happiest family times of the year.

"How about if we string popcorn and cranberries?" Rena suggested. "We could even make dough ornaments."

"Matt's eyes lit up for a moment. "I guess we could."

"You two go buy the tree, and I'll shop for everything else," Rena said.

"Would your father mind?" Joanna asked, although she really wondered whether they could afford it. Matt's father had sold a lot of his stocks and bonds. After the first week there had not been many prospective buyers for their house. And the sailboat had not sold yet either.

"Why should he mind?" Matt snapped, bitter. "He's not even going to be here for Christmas. He's going skiing in Utah."

Joanna wondered how his father could afford that. Matt was worrying if there would be enough money for him to go to college!

"Why don't we decide to have a wonderful Christmas?" Rena asked. "You know, just make that decision, and then do it."

"Okay," Matt said, without enthusiasm. "I decide to have a wonderful Christmas."

"Come on, Matt," Joanna said. "I second the motion. We're going to have a wonderful Christmas!"

Matt got up. "So I'll run upstairs and get into my old jeans; then we'll buy a tree."

Rena waited until he left. She sat down slowly on the stool next to Joanna. "I'm concerned about him," she said.

"Me too."

"I wonder," Rena began, thoughtful, "do you suppose he'd go to church with you?"

"With me? But I don't even go."

Rena raised an eyebrow. "I felt sure that you did."

"Why would you ever think that?" Joanna asked.

"Your eyes," Rena said. "Haven't you ever heard that saying, 'The eyes are the windows of the soul'? You can see quite a lot in people's eyes."

Joanna backed away a bit on her stool, not liking the drift of Rena's conversation, but she couldn't help asking, "What do you see in my eyes?"

Rena looked into her eyes for a moment. "A softness, a vulnerability that you don't hide nearly as well as you think. And a great yearning for love."

How could she see that? Joanna wondered, although she had a feeling about eyes, too. Some people would not look you in your eyes for anything. Some stared you down with hard, steely eyes. Most people did not really let you look too deeply into their eyes, as if they might reveal too much about themselves.

She suddenly remembered Melanie's violet eyes. They had frightened her somehow.

Rena smiled, and it occurred to Joanna that Rena's eyes were always open with a kind of wonder.

"I recognized your spirit, Joanna, the first day I met you. It's as if God told me to tell you how much He loves you. He wants you to put your life in His hands."

Joanna backed away, getting off her barstool without even knowing it. What a strange thing to say. "How would you know?" she asked.

"His children recognize each other's spirits."

Joanna looked away quickly. "Well," she said, "if I'm His child, why do so many bad things happen around me? Look at Melanie . . . and now Matt. And there's others. She thought about her father.

"Evil exists, too," Rena said. "There are bad spirits in the world . . . spirits of anger, suicide, lust, drinking."

Maybe she's crazy, Joanna thought, wanting to get away from the conversation, to run from the room, but she recalled her grandfather's telling her about Jesus. "My grandfather was a Christian," she found herself saying as she sat down warily one barstool away. "I was just a little girl, but I remember sitting with him looking at a sunset. He told me how much God loves us."

She looked at Rena for a moment. "When he talked about God, his eyes were bright, so full of light, like yours." She suddenly felt embarrassed. "Anyway, if there's a heaven, my grandfather must be there."

Matt came around the corner. "Hey, I don't need to hear any talk about dying! Come on, let's get the tree."

Joanna wondered how much he had heard.

She could feel Rena watching her as they left. Somehow she knew that Rena was praying for both of them, even with her eyes open.

It turned out to be a good day, Joanna thought that evening as Matt drove her home. He had finally ovecome his depression as they decorated the Christmas tree. They had laughed crazily with Rena. He had almost been the old Matt, and they had almost felt like a family.

When they drove up the road to her house, they saw that all the outside lights were on. There was a police car in the driveway!

"What could be wrong?" Joanna gasped as they rushed out of Matt's car. Then it began to dawn on her.

An ambulance siren wailed up the road toward them, and she and Matt raced to the house.

She threw the door open, then stopped when she saw them. Cathy's face and her mother's face were covered with blood, their clothing torn. Joanna screamed until Matt grabbed her and shook her.

Her eyes, wide with terror, turned to the wild man being subdued by the police in the family room. Her father!

"Lemme alone!" he shouted at the two policemen. "It's my house, my house!"

"Dad!" Joanna half whispered in horror.

As he turned to her, the policemen got a firm hold on him. "Damn, damn, damn you! You brought 'em. You brought damn cops!" His eyes were so glazed with anger that they frightened her more than his words.

"No, no, I didn't!"

He didn't seem to hear. He could barely get out the words. "I'll blacken your eyes—blacken your damn eyes! Boyfriend's, too!"

She hated him! She hated him! She had never hated anyone so much in her life!

"He's going to a hospital," her mother said, her voice shaking. "I can't take it anymore. I just can't take it! They know how to deal with alcoholics there."

"When did he start drinking again?" Joanna asked.

"I don't know," her mother said. "There's nothing I could do—I was just too weak . . ."

Matt turned to Joanna. "Guess I'd better go."

She didn't hear him.

Ambulance attendants rushed in, and before she knew what had happened, her father was gone. When it was all over and the police were leaving, she looked for Matt.

He was gone!

She knew in that moment that nothing, absolutely nothing would ever be the same between her and Matt again.

CHAPTER 12

At Santa Rosita High, Matt avoided Joanna between classes, and when they happened to pass each other, he pretended not to see her. Everyone knew that Joanna Stevens was not Matt Thompson's girl friend anymore.

During the first tearful days she thought that he didn't want anything to do with a girl whose father was a drunk. Then she remembered how he had tried to help Melanie, how his parents' divorce must have hurt him, how his back injury had ruined basketball for him. And now there were his father's money problems, too. She finally decided that Matt just could not face any more trouble—that was why he'd run out on her.

Someone said that he was taking Josie Jensen to a Christmas party, and Joanna thought she might die. How could he? Everyone knew Josie's bad reputation.

Over Christmas vacation Joanna began to buy bottles of wine and sherry when she did the family grocery shopping for her mother. The check-out clerks, busy with long lines of Christmas shoppers, didn't even ask for an ID.

By the middle of January she was rushing home after school for a glass or two of wine, unable to stop drinking. The check-out clerks still didn't question her as she bought more wine, even though the Christmas crush of customers was over.

The wine in her closet and under her bathroom sink disappeared so quickly that she couldn't believe she was drinking it all, and she had already taken as much of the wine and liqueurs from the kitchen cabinet as she dared.

Crying in bed at night, she would relive the wonderful moments with Matt. What was the sense in living without him?

In February, on Washington's Birthday, Matt called. At first she thought it was a daydream, but it was Matt. It really was him.

"Joanna?" he repeated as she stood speechless at the phone. "I've missed you so much." There was a quaver in his voice, and she knew that wasn't at all what he had planned to say. "Can we go somewhere tonight?" he asked nervously.

She stared at the phone. She must not sound too anxious. From the way he avoided her at school, she'd been sure that everything was over between them, yet she had never stopped loving him.

"Sure, Matt," she said, trying to sound calm. "Tonight is fine." She wondered if she had fooled him. She hadn't had a date with anyone during those terrible nine weeks, even though David had asked her to one of his church parties.

"How about a movie?" Matt asked.

"That's fine," she said, still trying not to sound anxious.

"I'll pick you up at seven," he said. "Bye, Joanna."

"Bye, Matt," she managed to say without giving away her joy. *He had missed her! He had missed her!*

"It was Matt!" she told her mother and Cathy. "He asked me out for tonight!" She whirled around with happiness.

Her mother smiled. "I thought that he might."

"I prayed about it for you," Cathy said.

"You prayed?"

Cathy nodded. "At Sunday school our teacher said

that prayer is the biggest power on earth. She said that God hears every prayer."

Joanna caught her mother's eye. She smiled and shrugged as if to say, She's little—humor her.

"I prayed for Dad, too," Cathy added. "Then he did come home from the hospital right after."

"That's nice, honey," her mother said as she started for the kitchen. "We'll eat early since you have a date, Joanna."

Cathy looked disappointed. "She doesn't believe me, but Dad did come home early, for Christmas, just like I prayed."

Joanna recalled Cathy's excitement when their father was allowed to come home early. It was as if she had expected a miracle and got it.

Well, their father had given up drinking. Yet something had gone out of him. He seemed sad, empty—even at Christmas. Either he brought home papers from his office and worked in the den evenings, or he watched TV. There was nothing happy about his life now, just when it seemed there should be.

Joanna patted Cathy's shoulder. "I think it's more that Mom prefers not to remember Dad being in the hospital."

It was better not to dwell on bad times, Joanna thought.

"I prayed for you and for Matt, too," Cathy said. "I asked God to touch both of your hearts."

Now where had she heard that? Maybe Cathy shouldn't go to that Sunday school; she could turn into one of those weird religious types, too. "Thanks, Cathy. I have to go wash my hair now."

She hurried to her room, nearly floating as she thought about Matt. What should she wear? What should she do with her hair? In her bathroom she was suddenly overcome with tears. She was going out with Matt again! He had missed her! She sat down on the bathroom floor, laughing and crying all at once.

She would have to be careful what she said to him. Maybe they would have to start all over again. She found her hands shaking. After opening the bathroom sink cabinet, she reached for the sherry. There was very little left.

After dinner she slipped into her new gold sweater and slacks, then glanced into the mirror. Her eyes were bloodshot. Well, eye drops would fix that. Eye drops, mouthwash, aspirin, antacid tablets. It had become a routine, a twice-a-day routine.

That evening, when she opened the front door, Matt smiled uneasily. "How are you, Joanna?" he asked.

She felt like a stranger. "Fine," she said, looking into his eyes. They stood there for a moment, just looking at each other, smiling shyly.

As they walked out to the car, she was surprised to see an old brown two-door Chevrolet.

"We sold the Corvette," he said, holding the door open for her. He sounded resigned to it all.

She didn't know what to say. "This car looks all right."

"Yeah. It's okay."

As Matt walked around the back of the car, Joanna felt as if this were their first date.

He slid into his seat, slammed the door, and turned to her.

"Oh, Matt," she said, "the car doesn't matter! I've missed you so much."

She was in his arms, tears rolling down her cheeks, remembering again how wonderful it felt just to have him hold her. Maybe she was throwing herself at him, but it didn't matter. Nothing mattered if she could only stay in his arms.

"I love you," he said. "I love you, Joanna."

He did love her! He did! She thought that her heart might burst with happiness. If it took all those weeks of agony to make him realize that he loved her, then it was worth it.

In the dim light they looked into each other's eyes and their lips met. His arms tightened around her until she thought she might be crushed. She didn't care.

When they finally moved away to catch their breath, his elbow touched the horn. It blasted out into the night for a second. They looked at each other in panic, then began to laugh.

"Maybe we'd better go," he said. He started the car. "Do you still want to go to a movie?"

"No," she said, "but maybe we should, Matt."

He nodded, then smiled at her. "Yeah. We'd better!"

The movie was a spy thriller, but Joanna could hardly follow the plot as she sat with Matt's arm around her, his other hand holding hers. She felt encircled with his love. He kissed her forehead, her cheek, her hand. She never wanted to be away from him again.

As they left the theater, Matt stopped at the drinking fountain in the lobby. He pulled a vial from his pocket and popped a pill into his mouth.

Joanna felt a stab of terror. He was still taking those drugs!

His hand slipped into hers as they walked out the theater door.

"Is your back still bothering you?" she asked.

"Yeah." He squeezed her hand.

"It's just that I'm worried that you might get hooked on those pills. You know the movies about drugs they're always showing at school."

"No nagging." He sounded angry.

She decided to drop the subject. Anyhow, his pills were prescribed by a doctor. She reached up to kiss his cheek. "Sorry. I promise, no nagging."

He looked down at her tenderly. "You'd better not."

She knew that it was an order. She had better not mention anything about his taking those pills again.

"You want to go to Morelli's for pizza?" he asked.

"Sounds great," she said, determined that they would have fun tonight, no matter what.

They headed across the parking lot for Morelli's blinking Christmas lights that were left up all year. The red sign, PIZZA, glowed through the night across the far end of the shopping center.

She wondered if anyone from school would be there. Probably. Morelli's pizza, spaghetti, and lasagna, the best in town, attracted everyone—high school kids, college groups, and families.

She and Matt stepped into Morelli's dimly lit entry.

The place was crowded as usual.

As they waited for the hostess, Chad stood up at a distant table and waved them over. There were eight kids from school at the long table, but room for two more.

"You want to sit with them?" Matt asked.

She wasn't certain that she did, but Matt looked as if he wanted to. "Why not?" she said.

She would rather have him to herself, she thought as she started for Chad's table, but the popular crowd had hardly noticed her since she and Matt quit dating.

She smiled at them. "Hi!" It was just the moment for them to see that she and Matt were together again, that he was crazy about her.

Curiosity danced in everyone's eyes as Matt seated her. She smiled up at him. "Thank you, sir."

"You're welcome, my lovely."

Their eyes met and held for a wondrous moment so full of love that she knew anyone who might be watching would know that Matt loved her.

As Matt sat down, Chad poked her with his elbow. "I didn't think anyone would ever make old Matt look like that again," he whispered.

She smiled, although she did not like Chad's word *again*. It only reminded her that Matt had once looked like that at Melanie. If only everyone would forget about Matt and Melanie!

Matt slid his arm around Joanna's shoulder and gave her a squeeze. Was he jealous of Chad's whispering to her?

She turned to Matt and, from the look in his eyes, thought he might kiss her there, right in front of everyone. Then he backed off, aware that the waitress was hovering over them for their order. His lingering smile touched Joanna's heart. She had never had anyone love her so much that he let everyone else around know it, too.

Glancing at the people at the table, she noticed that the girls looked jealous; the boys, curious.

Chad's date, Sue Martin, was last year's prom queen. Josie Jensen, whom Matt had taken out over Christmas vacation, was there with Tad Johnson, captain of the football team. Two of the girls, Teri and Sally, were cheerleaders. Their dates, Tom Hogan and Ron Saager, were stars of the basketball team.

If she had chosen who might see her with Matt tonight, she couldn't have done better. These were just the right people to see them together.

She felt Matt put his arm around her again and nearly melted as he gently held her hair away from her ear and whispered. "You're the most beautiful girl here."

"You're crazy," she whispered back laughingly.

He shook his head, and she could see that he

141

meant it. He really meant that she was the most beautiful girl there. Maybe it was true that love blinded people. She glanced at Josie, Sue, Teri, and Sally. She wasn't as pretty as any of them, but Matt thought so! She wondered if he thought she was more beautiful than Melanie had been.

As they sat there, eating pizza and laughing, Joanna couldn't help looking at Matt over and over to be sure this wasn't a dream. She found him looking at her with that same question in his eyes.

Later, as they got up to leave, Ron Saager said, "We're having a big keg blast at my house tomorrow night. Can you two make it?"

Matt glanced at Joanna, and she nodded. It seemed almost as if they didn't even need words anymore.

"Sure," Matt said, although he never took his eyes off Joanna.

Later, after they had eaten and the group was breaking up, Matt whispered, "Let's go to my house. No one will be home."

Fear flickered through her, but as his arm tightened around her waist, she didn't care what happened. She only wanted to be in his arms. "Okay," she said.

In the dimly lit parking lot they stopped by her car door. He leaned down and kissed her tenderly, then again with a longing she had never felt from him before.

"Hey, what is this?" Tad Johnson said with a laugh as he and Josie passed by, going to their car.

"This scene is better than the movies," someone else said.

"Never mind," Matt said to them. "They're just jealous," he whispered to her. Then his lips touched hers again.

For a moment she wondered what Josie Jensen

142

thought, then forgot about Josie, Tad, and everyone else.

When Matt finally moved away, he said, "Wow! Let's go!"

In the car she could sit right next to him, his arm around her. "At least it's better than a car with bucket seats," she said, thinking about the red Corvette.

"That's the only good difference," he answered, leaning down to kiss her hair.

As they drove up Matt's street, she wondered if his father or Rena might come home unexpectedly, but the house was dark except for the lights by the front door.

Inside Matt headed for the den. "Let's have a drink and watch TV," he said.

"Great!" She needed a drink. She glanced with him into the bar refrigerator.

"Looks like Dad left a whole pitcher of margaritas."

"What's that?"

"A Mexican drink. Tequila and something. You want to try it?"

She wasn't sure. She was not going to drink hard liquor. "Is it strong?"

He laughed. "Like lemonade."

"Okay, why not?" she said.

She helped him carry glasses, peanuts, and napkins to the coffee table in front of the brown leather couch.

He put the frosty pitcher on the table in front of them and turned on the TV. "What do you want to watch?"

"It doesn't matter," she said. All she wanted was to be with him. She poured the margaritas into their glasses and tasted hers. It was good. She took a long drink and felt the familiar warm glow spreading all

143

over her body. She filled her glass to the top again, smiling at Matt as he came to her.

"I love you, Joanna," he said.

She opened her arms to him.

It was two o'clock when they realized how late it was. They had drunk the whole pitcher of margaritas.

Joanna giggled as she tried to stand up. "Do you think we drink too much?"

Matt got up and was tottering, too. "And we're going to a party tomorrow night!" he said.

They looked at each other helplessly and dissolved into laughter.

"You know, you're even more beautiful when you laugh," he said, leaning down for another kiss.

She ducked away and ran for the front door. "I've got to get home. My mother will have a fit."

He chased her to the car, laughing, and she didn't know when she had ever been so happy. Everything was perfect. What could possibly go wrong?

CHAPTER 13

Despite a hangover, Joanna rushed through her Saturday housecleaning chores in the morning so she could spend the afternoon with Matt at the Santa Rosita Public Library. She had a term paper due in U.S. history. His paper was in American government.

The phone rang at one o'clock.

"Telephone, Joanna!" Cathy called out. She grinned as she gave the phone to Joanna in the hallway. "It's Matt," she whispered, her hand carefully over the mouthpiece.

Strange, Joanna thought, taking the phone. Matt was due right now. "You're going to be late," she guessed laughingly.

Matt seemed to miss her humor. "I can't take you to the library after all," he said. "Dad thinks we have a buyer for the sailboat. He wants me to help him show it in half an hour."

During the nine weeks they had been apart, she hadn't thought much about the sailboat's being for sale or whether or not it had been sold. All that she could think to say was: "I'll miss you."

At least they would be going to Ron Saager's keg party together tonight, she thought when she drove to the library alone. She hoped that if Matt's father did sell the sailboat today, it wouldn't put Matt in a bad mood for the party.

After dinner she changed into her new jeans and

burnt orange sweater. She hoped it was the right outfit to wear to a keg party since she had never been to one.

Just as she was ready, Cathy knocked on the bedroom door. "Matt's here! Dad's talking to him."

Joanna rushed down the hallway and saw with relief that Matt and her father were having a pleasant conversation in the family room. Lately her father had been more agreeable, as if he were trying to make up for the horrible problems he had put all of them through. Still, she couldn't forgive him.

Her mother was just stepping into the family room, too.

"Hi," Joanna said as Matt's eyes turned to her.

His face lit up. "Hi," he answered.

In the silence her whole family was looking at them as if they knew that something special had happened, as if they sensed that Joanna and Matt loved each other.

Later, as they walked to the car in the darkness, Matt asked, "Do you think everyone can see we're in love?"

She looked up at him with a smile. "I hope so."

Matt laughed, turning to her for a kiss.

It was then that she first noticed the smell of alcohol on his breath.

"You sold the sailboat," she guessed as they climbed into his old brown Chevrolet.

"Yeah. How did you know?" he asked.

She was not going to tell him that she knew because he had been drinking—that he was trying to make himself forget with liquor. She shrugged. "I just had a feeling that you'd sell it today."

"Let's not talk about it," he said as he drove down the road.

She remembered seeing him out on the dock with the sailboat, the breeze blowing his hair, the sun shining on him as if nothing would ever change. He had taken her out sailing with him two magnificent Sundays last fall. How he had loved that sailboat!

She moved closer to him on the front seat, and he squeezed her hand.

As they pulled out onto the main road, she recalled the first time he had picked her up at the school bus stop. How much fun he had been then. But that was before Melanie's suicide and before his father's money problems.

"Where does Ron Saager live?" she asked, hoping to make Matt forget about the boat.

"Santa Rosita Hills."

She darted a glance at him, wondering if driving there reminded him of his old house or of Melanie. There seemed no way of getting Matt away from his problems.

She was grateful, at least, that basketball season was finally over. Ron was star of the basketball team now that Matt couldn't play. The team had not made it to the play-offs this year without him. Would most of the team be at the party? She hoped not. They would only be another sad reminder for Matt.

As they pulled into Ron's driveway, Joanna was surprised to see an old brown shake house, not at all pretentious.

She brushed her hair hurriedly as they drove around back where the other cars were parked. "Looks like a big party," she said.

Music throbbed into the darkness from the building behind the house. "It's their old stables," Matt explained. "When they sold their horses, they converted the stables into a guesthouse and party rooms. It's a great place to party."

Joanna was glad that she'd worn jeans; everyone else getting out of cars looked very casual.

As she and Matt walked into the converted stables, the party was going full blast. A few kids were dancing to the wild beat of the music, but most of them congregated around the keg, glass beer mugs in hand. The sweet smell of grass hung in the air.

"Hey, Matt! Joanna!" Ron called out, and soon everyone was greeting them.

Joanna could feel people looking at her, some surprised that she and Matt were together again. Others must have heard about them from the group at Morelli's last night.

Matt handed her a frosty mug of beer. "It's all they have to drink," he whispered.

She had not really liked beer when she tried it at Matt's house one afternoon, but she decided then that she would learn to like it. She smiled up at Matt and took a sip. "It's good," she said. It was, maybe because it was keg beer and she was so thirsty.

"Hi, Joanna." It was Sue Martin smiling at her.

"Hi, Sue."

Nearby Josie Jensen, her black sweater and slacks far too tight, smiled up at Matt as if Joanna didn't exist. Josie's blond hair fell in soft waves to the shoulders of her black sweater. Her big blue eyes swam with secrets as she looked at Matt.

Joanna felt a surge of anger. First it had been Melanie, now girls like Josie after Matt. Joanna gulped her beer.

Matt smiled as if he knew she was jealous. "You want another beer?"

"Not yet." Her mug was still more than half-full. She was surprised to see that Matt had already downed his mug of beer.

He started for the keg. "I'm getting another."

She saw Josie turn to follow him, her hand reaching intimately for his arm.

"Matt! Just a minute." Joanna drank the rest of her beer as she hurried behind him. "I'm coming."

Josie stopped to talk to someone else, but her cheeks dimpled with amusement as Joanna passed.

Josie would make a play for Matt as soon as she

148

grew tired of Tad Johnson, Joanna thought. Josie collected boyfriends as if they were blue ribbons at a fair.

Matt waited until Joanna caught up.

She suddenly wished that Matt would hold her hand, but he was too busy talking to everyone else around them. Tonight it took an effort to look as if she were having a good time.

As he filled their mugs, Chad winked at her.

Joanna smiled, wondering if he had seen the whole episode with Josie. Chad never seemed to miss much.

Matt must have noticed that something was odd. His attention shifted to her, although she wasn't sure if it was because of Chad or because everyone was talking about the final basketball game of the season. It had been a wild overtime, the game of the season. Unfortunately Santa Rosita High had lost.

Matt led her to the long wooden bench lining the back wall of the room. "Still love me?" he whispered as they sat down. He slipped an arm around her shoulders.

"Usually," she said with irritation. She was surprised that her annoyance with him and Josie had surfaced like that.

He was taken aback, too. There was a long silence. Then he said, "Joanna, I want you to stay away from Chad. I heard about him chasing you at Melanie's party. I know he's been watching you."

Well, what about you and Josie? she wanted to say, but she didn't.

"You're my girl," he whispered, tightening his arm around her shoulder.

She smiled at him and sipped her beer. If Chad was so interested in her, why hadn't he called for a date when she and Matt weren't dating? All that time Chad had kept a cautious distance away in lit.

class. Was it because he and Matt were old friends?

She looked up at Matt. Whatever had happened, it was nice to see Matt jealous!

"What's wrong?" he asked.

"Nothing now." Her love must have shown in her eyes, though, because suddenly his lips were warm on hers. Oh, she did love him so! Yet it seemed as if one of them always had to love more than the other did. She felt as if she were usually the one who loved most.

She pushed him away gently. "Not here in front of everyone."

"Later?" he asked, and she nodded, smiling. Maybe that way they'd leave early, getting away from girls like Josie.

Strange. Joanna had never thought that Matt would be interested in a girl with Josie's reputation. Was it because Melanie had gotten herself into such trouble? Was Melanie's suicide why Matt never tried to go farther than kissing and hugging her? But what about Josie?

He got up with a grin, pulling her up, too. "Well, if we're not going to make out, let's drink."

Joanna laughed.

The rest of the evening he stayed close to her, occasionally glancing at Chad. There should be no question in anyone's mind: Matt Thompson was hers, even when he had too much to drink.

During the next month there was a keg party every weekend at a different house. None of the kids' parents were ever around during the parties, but why worry her family about that? Joanna thought. Anyhow, her mother was too busy with working now, and her father had turned inward, as if he didn't care. Cathy was the only one really interested in Matt and the parties.

150

"I'm going to have to have a party at my house before it's sold," Matt said one day at school. "Maybe the first weekend in April. The weather will be better, and we can have it out on the patio by the ocean."

"What about your father?" she asked.

"He'll be in Hawaii on business then."

"Wouldn't Rena have a fit?"

Matt shrugged. "I don't think she'll be there. I heard her on the phone—" Someone interrupted them, and Matt never finished what he was going to say.

The next day after school Matt was upstairs getting a book from his room when Joanna saw Rena.

"I'm afraid that I'm moving to Los Angeles," Rena told her. "Since the house is for sale, I've felt I have to keep my eyes open for a job."

Joanna knew that Rena needed to work. She was a widow and had very little money. It always amazed Joanna to see how happy Rena was, as if nothing bad had ever happened to her, as if life were an adventure.

"The realtors say that the house will probably sell soon," Rena said. "I know Matt and his father will find a beautiful condo to live in. They won't need me to help run things anymore."

Joanna knew how Matt dreaded moving to a little condominium. "I don't know how Matt will take that," she said.

Rena's eyes turned golden with light. "Will you hold my hands and pray for Matt?" she asked.

"No, thanks. I'd rather not," Joanna said stiffly. She escaped to Matt in the kitchen as quickly as she could, but Rena had already closed her eyes in prayer.

Thank goodness Rena was leaving.

Rena was gone by the first of April.

"At least the house is clean," Joanna said the Saturday afternoon of Matt's keg party. Matt's father still had a cleaning woman once a week so the house would be presentable for prospective buyers. "All we have to do is get glasses."

"No. The Keg Place furnishes the beer mugs, too," Matt explained. He had called The Keg Place and ordered beer two weeks ago simply by charging it to his father's credit card number. They would deliver the kegs of beer and the mugs anytime now. Matt said that his father's accountant at work would never even ask about the bill.

"Do you want me to buy pretzels and chips?" Joanna asked.

"Great. Then I can hang around for the keg delivery."

It made her feel a bit shy, helping with arrangements for a party at Matt's house. If Matt had had a mother around, she probably would not have wanted a girl friend playing hostess. Or maybe he wouldn't be having a drinking party at all.

The kitchen phone rang, and Joanna looked to see if Matt was going to answer it. He was sneaking a pill at the kitchen sink. Whenever she caught him taking the pills now, she pretended not to notice—it wasn't worth an argument.

She picked up the phone. "Thompson residence."

There was a slight pause, then a girl's voice asking for Matt. Joanna was sure it was Josie Jensen. Of all the nerve, she thought, handing the phone to Matt and turning away.

"Sure," he was saying. "Come anyhow. Don't worry about it."

When he hung up, he said, "Tad can't come. Josie wondered if she could come without a date."

"Oh," Joanna said, trying to look as if she didn't

152

care. "Well, great." She grabbed Matt's car keys from the kitchen counter. "I'll go get the pretzels and chips."

In the car she decided not even to think about Josie. It was too beautiful a day to be upset, especially here where she could see the ocean from every street corner. Bursts of bougainvillaea bloomed against walls and fences; flowering trees blossomed pink and white from the March rains.

Joanna wondered how Matt would feel if he did move to a small condo. He never talked about it. In fact, he had never even mentioned the sailboat after the day his father sold it. And he never mentioned Melanie anymore. Maybe that was why he drank so much now.

By seven o'clock she and Matt had moved all the outdoor furniture to the back patio. The keg of beer and mugs were set up on the redwood table. As Matt put down his end of a redwood bench, she could see that he was in pain.

"You'd better take a pill for your back, Matt," she found herself saying.

"I already took more than I'm supposed to."

"Oh, Matt!" She thought he had been taking far too many of the pain pills for the last few weeks. And both of them had been drinking more than usual, too. She started to say something but saw a flicker of warning in his green eyes. "Okay," she said. "I won't nag."

He grinned. "Thanks."

They had stuck two signs on the house. Each said PARTY, and arrows on them directed everyone around back. As people began to arrive, Joanna rushed in to put on lipstick and give her hair a fast brushing.

Glancing in the guest bathroom mirror, she wondered if Matt still thought she was beautiful. He didn't mention it anymore unless she asked him.

She started back out to the party, then stopped at the den's sliding glass door.

Josie was arriving, her blond hair shining against the sunset. Her tight blue T-shirt matched her blue eyes, and she wore the shortest white shorts that Joanna had ever seen.

Matt's back was to Josie, and she tiptoed to him. Smiling, she caught him in a big hug.

Joanna could see Matt's eyes suddenly open wide as Josie pressed against him. Then he was laughing with everyone else as Josie slipped her arm around his waist as if they were just old buddies. Josie took a long drink from Matt's beer mug, then smiled up at him, her blue eyes soft with secrets again.

Joanna knew that being old buddies with Matt was not at all what Josie Jensen had in mind.

CHAPTER 14

Joanna felt as if everyone were watching her as she opened the sliding glass door and stepped out into the glow of the sunset. The orange and golden radiance hung over the patio, reflecting off the doors and the glass panels in the fence until they were all suffused with color and light.

Through the glow she saw Josie still had an arm around Matt's waist, and he had an arm casually draped over her shoulders. He didn't even look embarrassed, Joanna thought, fuming. He seemed to think there was nothing wrong about it. Nothing! He was enjoying every moment of holding Josie!

Joanna headed for the beer keg, trying to hide her anger.

"Looks like you need a beer," Chad said.

She hadn't even noticed him standing by the keg. He was right, though. She definitely needed a beer. She tried to concentrate on the foam rising in the glass mug as Chad filled it for her. She would like two beers—one to dump over Josie's blond hair and another over Matt's thick skull.

"Thanks," she said stiffly as she took the cold mug. His hand lingered on hers a moment too long, and she began to see how she could get even. She considered the idea, then smiled up at Chad.

"You know," he said, grinning, "you really turn me on."

Any other time she would have flashed him an indignant look and turned away, but she was so furious. Matt had said that she should stay away from Chad. Well, what about Matt's staying away from Josie?

She tried to make her smile even more inviting. Perhaps it wasn't fair to use him to make Matt jealous, but Josie was still hanging onto Matt as if she were his date. As if Joanna were the outsider!

"I hope you don't mind my hugging Matty," Josie called out across the crowd to Joanna. "We're old friends, aren't we, Matty?" She giggled and squeezed him.

Joanna darted them a phony smile, noticing that Josie was smoking a joint, but then so were lots of the others.

Everyone was waiting to see what might happen.

"Yeah, old friends," Matt said, smiling, finally trying to untangle Josie's arm from him.

What was wrong with Matt that he didn't see into Josie's game? He was supposed to be such a genius. Well, she would like to shake him until his brains rattled.

She turned to Chad and took a long sip of beer.

"Easy," he said. "Take it easy."

"Sure." She drained the whole mug of beer.

Chad took her mug and filled it again. "Matt's not the only guy in the world, you know."

She looked up at him. "I've been noticing," she said, trying to look unperturbed. She had to get away before she couldn't handle the situation anymore. "Want to go for a walk along the beach?"

His blue eyes widened in astonishment. "Why not?" He filled his mug so full that the foam ran down over the side and clung to the dark curly hairs on his hand.

She felt him following her through the crowd on the patio and hoped that Matt noticed.

As Chad closed the wooden gate behind them, she

156

could see that Matt had not noticed their leaving together at all. He was far too busy having fun with Josie. Well, plenty of the others had seen them. He would find out sooner or later!

Orange and gold streaks of sunset moved down, splashing their brilliance across the dark ocean, still faintly lighting the beach. As she and Chad walked down to the water, she wondered how she could feel so empty, so awful in the midst of such beauty.

She felt Chad's arm slip around her waist, and she quickly pulled it away, then reached apologetically to hold his hand.

"Am I moving too fast for you?" he asked, grinning as they started walking along the beach.

She knew he wasn't talking about how quickly he was walking. "I don't know."

She stopped and sipped the cool beer thoughtfully. Maybe she didn't know anything; maybe it was stupid to try to be good, to be Matt's girl. Maybe Josie's attitude was right: Do whatever you feel like doing. And not worry about anyone but yourself. She recalled discussing philosophy in her life education class.

"What's your philosophy of life, Chad?" she asked.

He laughed. "My philosophy of life? You're kidding!"

"No."

He looked at her quizzically, then shrugged. "All I'm really interested in is having a good time."

She felt his hand tightening on hers. "Would you like to kiss me now for fun?" she asked.

He stared at her against the brilliant sunset.

She looked down for a moment, kicking the sand, wondering what she was letting herself in for, then smiled up at him.

"Yeah," he said, hoarse. "I'd like to kiss you. I've been wanting to kiss you for a long time."

She felt as if she had trapped herself, but there

157

seemed no way to stop now. She turned her face up to him.

He nearly lifted her from her feet as he gathered her up to him; then his lips were hard against hers, pressing hers apart. What was she doing? she thought, frantic. She didn't love him at all!

She tried to push him away, but his shoulders were firm against her fists. As she finally pushed away, she saw that someone had come out after them. He stopped and stood, still as a pillar of stone, watching them.

"Damn!" Chad said. "It's Matt."

She stared at Matt for a moment, then ran wildly to him. She would explain how jealous he and Josie had made her. "Matt!" she shouted, but he was running for his house. "Matt! Wait . . ."

Her feet sank into the dry sand on the hilly incline to his house, slowing her, and she thought she would never catch up to him. "I have to talk to you, Matt," she yelled as he reached the patio gate.

He turned, his face red with rage. "There's no sense in talking. You're just like Melanie!"

She stopped, shocked and bewildered.

He opened the gate, glared at her as if he hated her, and was gone.

She walked slowly to the back of the fence and sank down on the sand. How could he compare her with Melanie? She and Chad had only been kissing. Matt must have seen her push Chad away, she thought, then remembered: He had probably seen her turn her face up for Chad's kiss, too.

Chad ambled over, "He must be mad."

She nodded. "Furious."

"I'd better talk to him." He looked out at the darkening sky, and for a long time there was only the roar of the ocean between them. "I'll tell him it was my fault."

158

"But it wasn't, Chad."

He laughed harshly. "I'll tell him women can't resist me."

Joanna tried to smile, without much success. "Thanks. But I don't think it'll do any good."

He shrugged, and she watched him disappear around the fence.

Closing her eyes, she could still hear Matt's voice. "You're just like Melanie." She remembered the day on the beach with Matt, the day he had heard about Melanie's suicide. He had loved her so much, and he had been in such agony.

Joanna thought that she felt now just as he had then. She wished that she could cry.

Couples slipped out from the enclosed patio now to sit on the sand, bringing their mugs of beer with them. She scooted away, around the corner of the patio wall where no one would see her. If only Chad could convince Matt to come out to talk. They could make up. She could already imagine herself melting into Matt's arms.

Her heart leaped as she heard his voice by the gate. He *was* coming out! He was coming to her! After getting up, she started around the fence.

Matt and Josie were hanging onto each other, Josie giggling softly as she looked up at him.

They didn't even see her, she thought, stepping back. If they did, they had looked right through her as if she were only a ghost from the past. They were carrying their beer mugs, heading out to the water's edge.

Stunned, she watched them for a long time as they walked along the beach, until they were out of sight beyond the cliff. The ocean's roar engulfed her, roaring louder and louder until it surrounded her like a black fury. He would be sorry! She would make Matt Thompson so sorry!

159

Chad plodded around the corner with two over-flowing mugs of beer. His shoulders drooped; his face was grim. "No luck. He says he doesn't care."

Joanna whirled away, trembling with hurt and anger.

He waited for a while. "You want your beer?"

She nodded, reaching for it. She had to hold the cold glass mug with both hands, they shook so. She looked up at him.

He stood there like a dejected sheepdog.

She was suddenly laughing, or maybe it was crying, except there were no tears. It was a long time before she could take a sip of beer with her lips quivering against the cold glass. Her throat stuck together so that she could hardly swallow the beer. Then, at last, she got it down. "It was fun while it lasted," she finally said to no one in particular.

Chad flopped down on the sand. "I wouldn't know."

She glanced at him. "Who's your date tonight anyhow?"

"I don't have one."

She drank deeply, then smiled at him in the last glimmering light. "You do now. If you want one."

He scooted over beside her in the sand. "You're crazy."

"Did you just figure that out?" She reached over to feel his square chin. It was smooth, but her fingers felt the tough dark beard that grew beneath the skin. "You've been shaving for a long time, haven't you?"

He caught her hand and held it to his chin. "Yeah."

They sat like that for a long moment. Then she made her decision. "Well, let's drink up."

He was still staring at her in amazement when she emptied her mug. "Come here," he said.

She giggled. "Why don't you come and get me?"

As his arms closed around her, she put her hands over her mouth and giggled. "I do believe that first I'd like a little more beer."

She remembered sending Chad for more and more beer all evening.

Hours later she found herself groggy, staggering across the hard wet sand at the water's edge with Chad. It was dark. There was only a sliver of moon in the starlit sky.

"You're drunk!" he yelled above the ocean's roar. "I told you it was too much beer!"

She didn't quite understand. "Where's Matt? I want to see Matt." She reeled, waves of nausea welling up to her throat. "I'm going to throw up!"

She vomited and sank down onto the sand, throwing up over and over. How had this happened? she wondered, then remembered. It was Matt's fault. He was the one who had started it all. He and that Josie!

She finally sat up.

Where was everyone? Where was Chad now?

She saw car headlights in Matt's driveway. They flooded the house, making it look like something from another planet. She got up shakily and staggered across the sand toward the lights.

She thought she saw Chad on the driveway. Then she did hear his voice. He sounded drunk, too. "Great party!" he was yelling.

Why was he leaving her? He had kissed her. He had kissed her a lot behind the fence. He said he'd been wild about her for a long time, that he had thought she was such a nice girl. That maybe Matt would be lucky this time.

She was suddenly crying.

Where was Matt? Oh, where was he?

She swayed and staggered around to the far side of the house so that no one would see her. Matt had shown her where they hid the key.

Fumbling with the key, she dropped it twice before

it slid into the keyhole. Then she was finally inside the house. She had to find Matt!

Her mind reeled as she tottered through the white laundry room to the gleaming stainless steel kitchen, then to the den. Glancing in through the door, she could hardly believe what she was seeing. She stood, swaying, holding onto the wall.

Matt was kissing Josie on the couch—on the brown leather couch where she and Matt had so often held each other.. . . on *their* couch!

"Matt!" she cried out, her voice breaking.

He glanced up at her over Josie's blond hair. "Get out!" he said. "You're kishing Chad, my friend Chad."

"I am not," she said, then remembered that she had. "It's your fault! Your fault, Matthew Thompson! You made me do it."

"Get out!" he shouted. "I'm kishing Josie."

Josie turned to her with a smug smile.

Well, she would not even talk to that slut. "Drunk! Matt Thompson's drunk!" Joanna screamed at him.

He laughed. "Eberybody's drunk. Eberybody's drunk."

"Take me home, Matt," she pleaded, tears suddenly rolling down her face. "Take me home."

"Go home yourshhelf, Melanie!" he yelled. "Go home, Melanie!"

Melanie! She wanted to tell him that she was Joanna, not Melanie! That Melanie was dead and maybe it was his fault, too. That she was glad she hadn't given him Melanie's note from her wastebasket! But he was looking at her so hatefully that she couldn't say a word.

Sobbing, she turned away and groped her way back to the kitchen. She had to get out of here. She had to get home. She would have to call someone, but not her parents. .

David. She could call David. He would be glad to

162

help her. He wasn't like Matt and Chad. She finally got the phone off the hook and dialed his number.

David answered sleepily.

"It's me, David," she sobbed, relieved to hear his voice. "Joanna." She concentrated very hard on sounding sober. "You've got to get me . . . from Matt's house."

There was a silence. Then he sounded wide awake. "I'll be right there, Joanna. Just hold on."

Her head spun as she finally got the receiver back in place. There was a mug half full of beer on the kitchen counter. Maybe she'd feel better if she drank it. Drinking always made her feel better for a while anyhow.

She gulped the beer quickly, then ran for the side door as the beer rushed back up her throat. Outside she vomited again.

She remembered crawling to the front curb, heaving dryly. David would find her, she thought, and the next thing she knew David was lifting her into his car.

He sat her down and patted her face. "Are you all right? Should I take you to the hospital?"

She felt her eyes fly open. "No! No hospital!" Everybody would know.

He buckled her into the seat belt.

"I knew . . . I knew you'd come," she finally managed to say. "Have go home . . . Have go home . . ."

She saw the forlorn look on his face and found tears rolling down her cheeks again. "I just drinking, David . . . just drinking beer." That was all she could remember until he was helping her out of his car at his house.

"Listen, Joanna, I can't take you home like this. I'll make you coffee downstairs." He nearly carried her to the side door, to the rumpus room where he had had the church party.

"Waf—waf your friends see me?" she whispered,

thinking she did not want to embarrass him in front of his church friends.

"There's no one here," he said, settling her on the vinyl couch. "Only my parents sleeping upstairs." He covered her with an afghan. "I'll go get you some coffee. I'll be back right away."

She shook her head at him, tears streaming down her face. "Matt doesh—doeshn't love me."

"God loves you, Joanna," David said, looking near tears himself. "God loves you."

"No, no . . ." God couldn't love me, she thought. The image of Chad kissing her on the beach came to her, then Matt standing there, watching them. She was awful. Matt didn't even love her now. How could God?

"God loves you," David insisted. "Now just stay here while I go for some coffee."

She watched him leave and glanced around, not sure where she was. Getting up, she staggered to the sliding glass door and looked outside.

There, shimmering in the starlit night, was the swimming pool. How lovely it looked. A silvery dark rectangle reflecting the sky.

She pushed the glass door open, little by little, until she could squeeze through. Slowly, slowly she tottered to the serene water. She had gotten to be a drunk, just like her father. Matt didn't love her anymore. She remembered him on the couch with Josie. He loved Josie now . . . he loved Josie.

Joanna stood beside the lustrous dark water; it gleamed like shiny black satin. Matt had called her Melanie . . . Melanie. Did he really think that she was Melanie?

If only she had shown him that note from Melanie's wastebasket, maybe this wouldn't have happened. Maybe she was being punished for her thoughtlessness, her selfishness. Could it be that

164

Matt was right? That somehow she was turning into Melanie?

She looked down at the dark water for a long time, and then she heard Melanie, she saw Melanie's face in the water.

Don't be afraid, Melanie whispered to her. *Don't be afraid.* Melanie was smiling at her. How beautiful she was. *Come, come with me. See how sorry Matt will be then.*

Slowly the darkness moved toward her, and she was falling like a star spiraling to earth from the night sky. The silvery darkness reached up to her, engulfed her. Warm, so warm. Warmth surrounded her like a soft blanket, soothing away her agony in a velvety blackness.

At the last instant she saw Cathy's horrified face. Cathy would never in her life forget this! Perhaps she would even follow!

I want to live, her mind screamed, but it was too late.

She was lying on the wet concrete, water rushing from her mouth as someone pressed on her back.

It was dark, but not as dark as in the water. Starlight. It was a starlit night. She shivered uncontrollably.

David . . . He was trying to save her. He was sobbing over her.

"David?"

"How could you, Joanna? How could you?" he cried.

"She was calling me," she whispered. She turned to look at him. "Melanie said I'd make Matt *so* sorry."

"Heavenly Father," David prayed, "we take authority over the power of Satan *now,* in the name of Jesus!"

"Was it the devil?" she asked. She tried to think. She was certain that she had heard Melanie calling from the dark water, and she had seen her. She had! "Melanie was so beautiful, and she sounded so wonderful."

David was praying, praying, praying as he lifted her. He carried her slowly across the yard to the rumpus room and finally put her down on the couch.

"It's too late—too late for praying," she tried to tell him as she lay down on the couch. God could never forgive her for whatever had just happened.

"It's never too late," David said. "Never! God loves you. He can forgive anything. You only have to speak to Him through Jesus."

"Through Jesus?" she asked, not quite understanding.

"You have to accept Jesus . . . just accept Jesus."

"I want to, David," she whispered. "I want to." She realized that it was the truth. "Somehow I've always wanted to, I think, but I never—I never really understood."

"Just ask Him to come into your heart, to forgive you and blot out the past. He'll do it, Joanna, but you have to ask Him." Tears were running down his face. "Do you want to get on your knees?"

She sat up on the couch weakly, but she wanted to get down on her knees. As she slowly knelt, water ran from her wet clothes, making a puddle all around her on the rumpus room floor.

"I accept Jesus," she whispered, crying. "I accept Jesus."

"Ask Him to come into your heart," David sobbed, kneeling beside her.

"Please come into my heart, Jesus," She begged. "Please come into my heart. Forgive me . . . forgive me my sins." She could hardly get the words out, yet she had done it.

After a while she looked at David and knew he was

praying for her. His shirt and jeans were dripping wet, and tears streamed down his cheeks, but his face was glowing with joy.

She thought that something miraculous should be happening, that God would do something, but she still felt wet and cold and aching and wretched. She waited for a long time. Then David looked over at her as if he expected something to be happening to her, too.

She did feel better, and David had said that God would forgive her. "I guess I'd better go home," she finally said, wiping her eyes.

CHAPTER 15

At two o'clock the next afternoon Joanna could hardly pull herself out of bed when Matt called. She was certain that she had never felt so awful in all her life.

She slowly began to recall David's sneaking her home last night. Luckily no one had seen her come in dripping wet and drunk.

Her mother looked worried as Joanna plodded out to the hall phone. "You must have the flu," she said. "You look so pale."

"I'll be all right, Mom. Don't worry," Joanna said, although she felt like a zombie. She wasn't even sure that she wanted to talk to Matt. She could still see him with Josie on the den couch.

Still, he had seen her kissing Chad, too. If only she could forget the whole miserable night. If only there was a way to erase it all, to start over.

Having picked up the phone, she managed a cool "Hello."

"I didn't know if you'd be talking to me," Matt said.

She didn't anwer.

"I should have cut off Josie right away," he said, "but I started drinking when they brought the keg. You know, when you went shopping. I'm sorry."

Just hearing Josie's name infuriated Joanna. She could still see Josie walking onto the patio and hugging Matt. Josie had made both of them look like fools in front of everyone else.

There was a long silence, and Joanna was determined not to be the one to break it. She could imagine Matt now, probably in that stainless steel kitchen, alone as usual.

The thought of his being alone began to melt her resolve. He was always alone now. "When did you want to see me?" she finally asked.

"Now?" he asked hopefully.

She felt too awful. She just wanted to go back to bed and forget everything. "No, not now."

"Can I take you to dinner at Morelli's?" He added, "Please, Joanna."

She wondered what had happened to Josie, but this was no time to ask. "Okay, Matt. But not until six o'clock."

As she hung up, she wondered if he didn't have a hangover, too. Of course, he hadn't tried to drown himself on top of drinking all of that beer.

The phone rang again as soon as she hung up. "Are you all right, Joanna?" David asked.

"I've been better," she admitted, embarrassed about last night. "Thanks for everything, David."

"I want to see you," he said, "but we're going to visit family friends. I can't get out of it."

"I'll be okay," she said, although she wasn't too sure, considering how awful she felt.

Hanging up the phone, she recalled telling her mother not to worry about her, too.

The house was quiet, wonderfully quiet. She could go back to bed, she thought, glad that Cathy was at Dede's house and wouldn't see her like this.

Matt looked angry when he picked her up, and she couldn't imagine why. He had been the one pleading with her to go out. When they were in the car, she realized he had been drinking again. He had been drinking a lot, maybe all day long.

170

"Let's kiss and make up," he said, his words slurring.

Joanna cringed. His breath smelled foul; his cheeks were flushed. She edged away to her door. "I'm sorry about what happened, too, Matt," she said. "It was stupid. We both were stupid."

"You don't look very sorry sitting on that side of the car," he said.

"It's just that my stomach is queasy, and you smell like a brewery."

"*You're* criticizing?" His green eyes flattened with anger, and he squared his jaw as he started the car. He pulled out onto the road so fast that the tires squealed. "*You* were pretty drunk last night yourself!"

"I'd like to forget the whole thing," she said. "I'm really sorry."

"It's hard for me to forget you and Chad," Matt said. "You're supposed to be my girl. Chad's supposed to be my friend!"

She decided not to answer. It wasn't going to be easy for either of them to forget. Maybe they would never get over last night.

Matt looked furious as he drove. "Can you imagine how I felt, seeing you two kissing on the beach?"

"It hurt me to see you with Josie, too."

He didn't seem to hear. "It almost killed me to see you with Chad!"

"It almost killed me to see you with Josie, too! She started the whole thing!"

Joanna was sorry she had said anything. Why couldn't they just make up? She looked at Matt. He was so hurt and angry. "Do you think we'll ever forgive each other, Matt?"

"I don't know," he said dully. He swung the car into a road overlooking a steep canyon.

"Where are we?" she asked, looking farther down

the road. There were cars parked in the shade of eucalyptus trees, and couples in the cars were wrapped in each other's arms.

"It's the water district road," he said.

She had a feeling that Matt had been here before. "Is this where you bring girls like Josie?" she snapped. She was sorry as soon as the words were out of her mouth.

Darting a furious look at Joanna, he parked the car alongside the road. He turned off the ignition and moved toward her.

She backed away.

"I only want something in the glove compartment," he said angrily. He reached into the glove compartment and pulled out a flask. "I need a drink. How about you?"

Joanna's stomach turned over. "What is it?"

"Bourbon."

She shook her head. She didn't know why she had asked in the first place. She didn't want a drink at all. Usually when she had a hangover, she needed a drink the next morning, but not today.

She watched him tilt the flask to his mouth, his Adam's apple bobbing as he swallowed. Today it looked disgusting. The smell of the bourbon made her stomach churn.

"Look, Matt, I don't want to sit here," she said. "I thought we were going to Morelli's."

He turned to her, his green eyes hard, as if he was daring her to make him leave. Finally he gulped from the flask again.

What had happened to the happy Matt he used to be? Had that all been an act? Sure, lots had gone wrong in his life, and she hadn't helped at all last night.

She took a deep breath. Okay, she would try again to make up. "Please forgive me about last night, Matt. I really forgive you." As she said the words, she began to feel that somehow they were becoming true.

"What's wrong?" he asked, his voice nasty. "You want a drink after all?" He pushed the flask at her.

"That's not it at all," she protested.

Ignoring her, he screwed the lid back on the flask and threw it into the glove compartment.

"Matt, I'm trying to apologize!"

He backed the car out wildly, then lurched it forward. As he floored the gas pedal, they went weaving onto the road.

"Stop this, Matt!" she shouted.

At the end of the road there was only a barbed-wire fence in front of a deep canyon. The car roared to it.

"Matt!" Joanna screamed.

Grinning, he squealed the car to a stop.

"Think I'd drive over the cliff?" he asked with a laugh as he looked out over the rocky canyon.

"Please don't be like this," she pleaded.

He was intent on the canyon below. "Maybe you don't know the real me," he said, his voice flat, strange.

She reached out and touched his hand. "I love the real you."

"Yeah?" He looked down at her hand on his as if he had never seen it before. Taking her hand, he squeezed it hard.

"You're hurting me!" She couldn't believe that he could be like this. It was as if he were two different people. She wondered how many pain pills he had taken today.

"Let's go to Morelli's," he said.

She felt a wave of relief for a moment. Then he drove away crazily, turning the car radio on to a wild rock station. She sat with her hands clenched into fists all the way to Morelli's.

Inside the restaurant, as they were being seated in

a window booth, Matt told the waitress, "We'll have a bottle of red wine."

"I don't want any," Joanna said quietly, "I guess I'll have a glass of milk."

Matt frowned at her.

"I'm afraid I'll have to ask for your ID," the waitress said to Matt.

Joanna watched in amazement as he dug for his wallet and pulled out his driver's license. He handed it to the waitress nonchalantly. What was he doing? He was seventeen. She knew that for certain.

The waitress looked at his license, then at Matt several times.

After she left, Joanna whispered, "How did you pull that off?"

He grinned. "I'm twenty-one."

This is ridiculous, she thought. She had seen his license. He was definitely seventeen.

"Okay, you're twenty-one," she said just to be done with the subject.

Matt did not want to drop the discussion. "It's a Tijuana Special," he said. "Your friend Chad and I went over the border for them last summer. In fact, it says I'm almost twenty-two."

Joanna wondered how much more she didn't know about Matt. He'd never told her about the phony license.

The waitress darted a suspicious glance at Matt when she brought the bottle of wine. It was far too quiet as she placed a wineglass in front of him and poured the red wine.

After she had left, Joanna whispered, "You didn't fool her."

Matt didn't answer, but his eyes raked her harshly, as if to say, Shut up! He downed the first glass of wine and quickly poured another, then dug out his pills.

Joanna stared at him. "Matt, you shouldn't."

He popped two of the pills into his mouth and swallowed them with the wine. "I've been doing it for months," he said. "Hasn't hurt me yet."

She didn't believe him. It was her fault that he was doing this. She had hurt him so badly last night.

After the waitress brought their pizza, Joanna tried to concentrate on eating, but she could hardly swallow.

Matt ate one slice of pizza, then sat there drinking wine.

They seemed to be sitting there forever, she thought, looking away from his glazed green eyes. She glanced around at the people in Morelli's, hoping that someone might stop by to pull Matt out of his mood, but it was still early. There were mostly families at the tables.

"Maybe we'd better go," she suggested after a while.

"Not done yet," he said, glancing at the wine bottle. It was still a third full.

She sat back. "Sorry."

He didn't answer. He stared strangely.

She would have to drive, she decided. She didn't have her driver's license with her, but that was too bad.

As he tried to pour another glass of wine, he bumped the goblet, nearly tipping it over. He set the bottle down hard. As he looked up at her angrily, his words slurred. "How'd you go home?"

He meant last night, she thought, not wanting to tell him about calling David. She started to get up. "Let's go home, Matt. I'm tired."

He stood up and, reaching over the table, pushed her down in her seat. "How'd you go home?"

"Let's talk about it in the car," she said, frightened. "Not here."

"Talking now!" he yelled, and people turned to stare at them.

175

"Please, Matt. Everyone is looking at us," she whispered.

He shouted, "Who took you home?"

She saw the waitress getting old Mr. Morelli from the kitchen. They were starting for their booth.

Joanna stood up. "Come on. Let's go home."

Mr. Morelli, usually smiling broadly under his thick black mustache, looked grim as he hurried toward them, his voluminous white apron still tied around his waist. "Everything all right here?" he asked.

"No!" Matt shouted. "She's my girl!"

Joanna tugged at Matt, certain now that everyone in the restaurant had noticed. Someone in a booth at the far wall was standing up to see what was going on.

"Very beautiful girl, too," Mr. Morelli said, helping Matt up. "I'd like you to have dinner on the house, you're such a handsome couple." He was expertly ushering Matt out by the elbow, smiling and talking pleasantly, while Joanna trailed behind them.

She could see people staring at them, disgust on their faces. As they approached the door, people waiting for tables gaped at them. She thought that they would never get outside.

Finally they were out, and Morelli's Christmas lights blinked at them in the darkness. "Thank you," she said to Mr. Morelli.

Matt looked confused for a moment, then saw where he was. "Hey—"

"Don't bother to come back," Mr. Morelli interrupted. "I could lose my license, lose the whole restaurant over a kid like you." He rushed back in, slamming the door behind him.

Joanna grabbed Matt's arm, trying to hurry him through the dark parking lot. "I'll drive," she said as they stopped on the driver's side of his car.

He stood digging in his pocket for the car keys for a long time. "I'm driving," he said, but he could hardly stand up.

"You never let me drive," she protested.

He slapped her face. "David picked you up!"

She held her burning cheek, backing away from him. "How did you know?"

"I guessed," he said, shoving her roughly into the car, past the steering wheel, and to the passenger side. "How dumb do you think I am?" His eyes were wild in the light of the open car door. He slammed it and started the motor. Rock music blared.

There was no time to fasten her seat belt before they lurched forward, then careered crazily through the parking lot.

"Please, Matt."

He peeled out onto the road and floored the gas pedal.

"Where are we going?" she shouted over the rock music.

"You go with nobody but me!" he yelled.

He sounded crazy, she thought, looking out. The road was completely dark. "Your lights! Turn on the headlights!"

He turned them on and glared at her as if it were her fault.

She tried to concentrate on the road ahead and was glad there was so little traffic. On the radio the rock singer wailed about how rotten love was, and Joanna agreed with him as Matt sped in the direction of her home.

He suddenly slowed down and whipped the car around a corner.

"Where are we going?" she asked, then recognized the road and the eucalyptus trees whizzing by in the headlight glare. It was the dead-end water district road leading out over the canyon.

The car was going faster and faster, flat out now.

"Matt!" she screamed. "Stop!"

He looked crazy, as if he weren't hearing her at all.

"No, Matt, no!" She grabbed his leg, pulling his foot away from the gas pedal.

Their headlights pierced the darkness, shining on the barbed-wire fence at the end of the road. It was too late to stop!

Joanna tugged desperately at the steering wheel, pulling it toward her as hard as she could, her mind screaming, *God help me, God help me!*

At the last moment she felt the car turning away from the canyon, turning, then suddenly flipping . . . flipping . . . She was against the door, flying out, somersaulting into the night, the car crashing through the darkness beyond her.

For a long time there was only gray shadowy silence.

When she finally opened her eyes, she saw fire flaring from the smashed car up a eucalyptus tree, lighting everything around them.

They had not gone over the cliff into the canyon!

After pulling herself up out of a brambly bush, she stumbled toward the flickering firelight. "Matt!" she screamed, holding her aching neck. Her head felt strange, as if it might wobble off her neck.

She nearly tripped over his body. "Matt, oh, Matt." She collapsed on her knees beside him. "Please, God, let him be okay," she prayed. "Please, God."

He was so still, sprawled out on his back in the weeds by the roadside. What could she do?

The crackling fire spread rapidly along the row of eucalyptus trees, each tree bursting into flames like a giant torch. She felt frantic. She had to do something.

Looking at Matt, so sweet and innocent as he lay there, she remembered David's prayer. "Please let him be alive, God. In Jesus' name I pray."

She kissed Matt's forehead and saw his lashes flutter. He was alive!

In the distance fire engines screamed through the night. Someone had seen the fire. Firemen would know what to do about Matt.

"It's okay, Matt," she said. "Everything's going to be all right!"

He tried to smile.

"We're alive, Matt," she said. "We're alive!"

She had never been so thankful in all her life. "Oh, God, thank you," she cried out, tears of gratitude welling in her eyes. "Oh, thank you, God, thank you!"

She felt a sudden glow in her heart.

"Forgive me, forgive me, God! Help me. Please help me! I'm an alcoholic. . . . And help Matt. We're both alcoholics, and Matt's hung up on drugs, too. Oh, God, we need you!"

A wondrous joy leaped through her until she knelt, enthralled, in a golden burst of light, aglow with love. For a long moment waves of love swept through her like torrents. She was surrounded by love, love as she had never felt it. And she knew, without even thinking, that this was God's embrace, that God had touched her with His love.

The words came to her from somewhere: "Therefore, if any man be in Christ, he is a new creation: old things are passed away; behold, all things are become new!"

With a strange clarity she understood that she would never be the same again, not now or through eternity. She knew that God had withdrawn her alcoholism as someone else might pull a sliver and that she was changing . . . changing.

The whole world around her shimmered in the golden light. She found herself on her knees, hands reaching joyously out to God in the night sky, as if she were part of a magnificent ancient rite. She knew she would never be as happy as this again all the rest of her earthly life.

She was still conscious, lying on the hard ground, when the fire engine and then, later, the ambulance arrived. As the white-suited attendants lifted Matt on a stretcher into the ambulance, Joanna whispered, "He's going to be all right."

The attendants looked at her strangely as they laid her on the stretcher.

She was smiling as the grayness moved toward her, smiling as everything became black.

CHAPTER 16

For a long time there was only darkness and confusion. Then Joanna saw the surge of light and heard the glorious singing. "Morning is broken, like the first morning. Blackbird has spoken, like the first bird. . . ."

Bells rang out joyously across the earth and heavens, echoing and reechoing from planet to planet, sunset to sunset, mountain peak to mountain peak. Her heart joined the clouds of choirs coming down in great light with Jesus.

"Joyful, joyful, we adore Thee, God of glory, Lord of love. . . ."

Jesus was coming to her, strong as a carpenter, His eyes welling with such loving tenderness. His arms moved out to her in welcome, and she knew, without hearing a word, that she was to follow Him.

There, in the multitude behind Jesus, was her grandfather smiling at her, and she remembered a song he had taught her when she was little.

She sang out loudly now, with all her heart, in offering to Him: "Oh, how I love Jesus. Oh, how I love Jesus . . ."

She was moving to Him now in the power of love, floating across earth, and she heard a wondrous voice saying, "This is my son, with whom I am well pleased."

She lifted her hands up to Him.

Let me go with you now, she thought. Let me go with you now!

She heard no voice, but she knew that it was not yet time to be with Him. There was work for her to do on earth. What it was, she did not know, but there was His work to do.

Why was she chosen after all the bad things she had done? Then He gave her the answer: His grace, His loving-kindness.

She heard her name: "Joanna! Joanna!"

Slowly, slowly He moved away, receding with the clouds of multitudes as easily as billowing fog moves over the sea.

She seemed to be going backward through a tunnel, away from the great light. When He was gone, there was only darkness. Yet she had never felt such peace and happiness in her life.

"Joanna? Joanna?" her mother called out, her voice quavering.

She opened her eyes and saw her parents and David hovering over her hospital bed.

David was beaming at her.

Her mother's and father's eyes were red, full of tears.

A nurse leaned over from the other side of the bed to look at Joanna's eyes. "It's not often that our patients wake up singing. Can you put your arms down, Joanna?"

She was suddenly aware that her hands were still raised to Him. She lowered them slowly, remembering again His look of loving-kindness.

"What was I singing?" she asked. She was surprised at the new sound of her voice. It was soft now, loving, a musical sound.

"Something about Jesus," the nurse said, her eyes full of wonder as she took Joanna's pulse.

"You were singing 'Oh, How I Love Jesus,'" David said. He turned to the nurse. "Do things like that happen often in hospitals? You know, religious things?"

The nurse shook her head slightly, as if she were still stunned. "Sometimes. You know, when people are on the edge, surprising things can happen." She suddenly seemed to remember her job and started out. "I'll notify the doctors. And I'll tell Cathy out in the waiting room, too."

"What did the nurse mean, 'on the edge'?" Joanna asked.

Her mother blinked hard, turning to Joanna's father. She sobbed as he took her in his arms.

Her father cleared his throat, but his words trembled. "The doctors didn't think you'd live, Joanna. Not one of them thought you had a chance for the last two days."

He glanced at David. "David prayed and prayed for you. And Cathy's probably still praying now. Even your mother and I prayed."

Joanna remembered. "I saw Grandfather for a moment, just a moment. He looked so happy and so beautiful. That's why I sang it, you know, 'Oh, How I love Jesus.' Grandfather taught me that."

Her father nodded, his eyes thoughtful. "He taught me that a long time ago, too."

"Did you see Him?" David asked, and she knew that he meant Jesus.

She closed her eyes and could see Him again in her memory. "Yes, I saw Him. He was so beautiful, so tenderhearted, so full of love." She thought for a moment. "But I don't know why He chose me. I just don't understand."

"Jesus explained it in the Bible," David said. " 'The wind bloweth where it listeth, and thou hearest the sound thereof, but canst not tell whence it cometh, and whither it goeth: so is every one that is born of the Spirit.' "

Yes, she thought. God's spirit had come to touch

her heart like a great wind that appeared from nowhere. No one knew where a wind came from or where it might go next.

Her life was connected to the Bible, she thought, astonished. She tried to recall exactly how it had happened.

First, she had accepted Jesus at David's house. And she had knelt in thanksgiving at Matt's side as he lay by the road, thanking God that Matt was still alive, thanking him so joyously. And then, like a great wind, God's loving spirit had come upon her.

"Can it happen to everyone?" she asked David.

He nodded. "If they open their hearts and accept Jesus. It's not always such a dramatic conversion like yours. Usually it comes slowly, being attracted more and more to Jesus."

Her father's voice was reflective. "Your grandfather said it came slowly to him. He said he was drawn to Jesus until being a Christian was the most important thing in his life."

Then that's what has been happening to Cathy, Joanna thought.

"It's a great wonder, no matter how it comes," David said.

"David says it's what people call being born again," her father said.

"Except that most people don't really know what *born again* means," David said. "I think it's one of those things like love or sadness or pain. You don't know what it is until you have it yourself."

"It's a wonderful glow of . . ." Joanna struggled to find the right word.

"Power?" David suggested.

"Yes," she said. "Power. It's a wonderful glow of God's power. It blots away everything bad you've ever done and fills you with so much love. It's His love. And then you can somehow love everyone else, too."

She remembered the beautiful moment she had been held in God's hands. "I feel so full of joy and peace."

"That's what my—my sister said years ago," her mother said. "But when Annie quit taking her heart medicine and put herself in God's hands—and died"—she was suddenly crying—"I fought and fought religion. I fought God."

Joanna reached for her mother's hand. "So did I!"

"I think that everyone does," David said.

"I see now how crazy that is," Joanna said. "I've never felt so happy in my life. And somehow I know I'll never be lonely, that He'll always be with me if I just let Him."

She thought for a moment and couldn't help smiling. "When I think how important it seemed to be popular . . ."

Her parents could only stand there, looking at her through teary eyes, shaking their heads with loving wonder.

She was smiling when she slowly drifted off to sleep.

Hours later, when she awakened, they were still there.

Noticing the unusual brightness in her father's eyes, she understood. "You're going to be fine now, Dad," she said, as certain as if God had told her, as if He had given her wisdom. She knew, too, that she had forgiven her father for his drinking and what it had done to their family; her hatred for him was gone.

He caught her hand and held it. "When the doctors said that you probably wouldn't live, that it would take a miracle, I promised—" He couldn't go on and held his handkerchief to his trembling lips for a long time. "I promised God that if you lived, that if you would be all right again, I would never touch alcohol for the rest of my life."

She squeezed his hand, her own eyes bright with tears, and reached for her mother's hand. Joanna put their hands together, and they were suddenly in each other's arms.

David smiled at her, embarrassed. "Heidi called. She sends her love."

Joanna dimly remembered the afternoon she and Cathy had gone riding with Heidi. Heidi must have sensed that something was terribly wrong with them that day, and she had tried to help them forget.

Someday, Joanna thought, Heidi was going to need help. Someday she was going to have to face people instead of horses. Joanna felt ready to be her friend.

She suddenly recalled the accident. "How is Matt?" she asked.

Her parents and David glanced at each other as if they didn't know whether or not they should tell her.

She had been so certain that he would be all right. It didn't seem possible, she thought as she finally asked, "Is Matt dead?"

"No," David answered. "He's still alive. But the doctors aren't sure that he'll live. If he does, they say he'll never walk again. He'll always be in a wheelchair."

"It's his spine," her mother explained. "He's paralyzed from the neck down."

Strange, Joanna thought. She had been so convinced that he would be all right. "Do you suppose that the doctors might be surprised again?" she asked.

It wasn't until two days later that Joanna's doctors allowed her to walk down the hospital corridor to the intensive care ward. She wore the new yellow robe that Cathy had chosen for her, as bright yellow as her new joy.

"Only five minutes," the nurse warned Joanna as she led her around to Matt's curtained cubicle.

She nearly gasped when she saw him. He hung upside down in a Stryker frame, a hideous slinglike contraption, face down toward the white tile hospital floor.

"Matt," she whispered, bending down.

His green eyes opened with recognition, then closed, as if he did not want to see her or anyone else.

"Please, God," she prayed, "let me say the right words to Matt. He looks so unhappy, so bitter."

She got down on the cold floor, lying nearly under him so she could look up into his face.

His eyes were still closed, but his lips trembled.

"God loves you, Matt," she said. "He loves you."

Matt's voice was hard, taut with bitterness. "I'm being punished. I'm being punished for Melanie . . . for trying to kill you and myself . . . for all the rotten things I've done in my life."

She shook her head, looking up at him. "You're punishing yourself. You're sinking yourself in guilt. God can forgive anything . . . anything!"

He had to understand that God loved him. He could die any minute. "God will forgive you, Matt," she said, "but you have to forgive yourself, too."

He looked as if he might cry. "Do you forgive me, Joanna?"

"Of course, I forgive you. I forgive you with all my heart!"

Matt opened his eyes. Hope glimmered in them.

She wanted to cry for the pain he had been going through the past few years. He thought that no one loved him. Not his mother and sisters—they had moved away. Not his father, who was too busy. Not Melanie, who had killed herself. And then not even Joanna!

"Do you really forgive me?" he asked with a catch in his voice.

Her eyes were wet with tears. "If God can forgive us anything, then how can I not forgive you?"

He smiled, a thin smile, but a thoughtful one.

"I'm guilty, too, about Melanie," Joanna said. "That night at her party I found a strange note in her wastebasket. I even wondered if it might be a suicide note."

How long ago that seemed now, she thought, looking away across the white tile hospital floor. But she had to go on; she had to make Matt understand.

"You see, I was guilty, too. I should have told you about her note—you might have saved her. But I didn't tell you, and it tormented me. I think that's part of why I started drinking too much. I was trying to hide my guilt."

She looked up at him again. "Maybe that's why you started taking so many pills and drinking so much. You felt full of guilt, too."

"Maybe," he whispered. He sounded as if he didn't want to think about it.

"But God has forgiven me," she explained. "Melanie was responsible to God for her own actions, too. Not just you and me responsible for her."

It was so important that he had this right. "Do you understand, Matt? Melanie was responsible to God, too, just as you and I have to answer to Him for our own selves. Each person has to get right with God."

"Yeah," he said. Then his voice was full of anguish. "But I tried to kill us! I tried to kill both of us!" He looked horrified, as if he could see it all again.

"God will forgive you even that," she insisted. "He loves us so much that He will forgive anything if we are truly sorry." She was surprised at her new understanding. It was as if God had given her His wisdom.

"He loves you, Matt," she said again.

There was a long silence. Then his lower lip quivered. "Thanks . . . for turning the . . . steering wheel," he whispered.

Her eyes filled with tears of joy. "Oh, Matt, I'm so glad you're thanking me for it! It means you're glad we're alive!"

He looked at her closely. "Something's happened to you. You look different . . . more beautiful than ever before. It's your eyes."

She beamed. He could see it! He could see her joy! Even here on the cold hospital floor!

"The doctors call it a miracle," she said. "They didn't think I'd live, but God healed me." She thought for a long time, then prayed before she said, "It can happen to you, too."

Eyes brimming with tears, his whisper was as much to himself as to her: "It's going to take a miracle."

"Yes," she answered softly. "It *is* going to take a miracle. But miracles do happen."

He smiled ruefully at her. "You know," he said after a while, "your eyes look like Rena's now."

Joanna wanted to kiss him for the sheer joy of the idea. Rena, oh, Rena, she thought, remembering the first time she had seen her. Rena had been reading by the big oceanfront window. She must have been reading the Bible because her eyes had been luminous, so golden with light and love. Did her eyes really look like Rena's now?

She remembered Rena's saying, "Eyes are the windows of the soul."

"It's the joy in our eyes, Matt," Joanna said. "It's the wonderful, wonderful joy in being a child of God."

She saw the nurse coming. "One more minute, please?"

The nurse nodded.

"I have to go, Matt, but we have time to pray. Will you pray with me? Please, will you pray?"

He looked hopeful despite tears that dropped straight down and splattered on the white tile floor near her face. "Yes, Joanna," he said with a wonder-struck catch in his voice. "Please, let's pray."

ELAINE L. SCHULTE was born and raised in Crown Point, Indiana. She has written numerous short stories and articles that have appeared in magazines and newspapers around the world. A recent novel, ZACK AND THE MAGIC FACTORY, appeared on television. She lives with her husband in Rancho Santa Fe, California. They have two sons in college.

About WHITHER THE WIND BLOWETH, Mrs. Schulte says, "While at a librarians' banquet, the words 'whither the wind bloweth' came to me so strongly that I felt it was meant to be my next novel. No one had said the words; the librarians at my table had never heard them. They looked at me strangely when I told them that perhaps my next novel had begun. Unfortunately, I couldn't start a novel then. A year later, as I stepped into a strange chapel, an elderly black man was speaking from his pew. As I moved to the pew behind him, I heard the end of his testimony: 'whither the wind bloweth.' I knew then that it was time to begin writing. While I wrote WHITHER THE WIND BLOWETH, the words poured out of me as never before. It was as mysterious to me as how the title was given, as mysterious as from whither the winds blow."

FLARE ORIGINAL NOVELS
FOR YOUNG ADULTS
By
KAREN STRICKLER DEAN

Ms. Dean, a former dancer, conveys the excitement and discipline of the dance world to her readers.

MAGGIE ADAMS, DANCER   80200/$2.25
Maggie Adams lives in a dancer's world of strained muscles and dirty toe shoes, sacrifices and triumphs, hard work and tough competition. She has little time for anything but dance, as her family and boyfriend come to learn. Her mother spoils her, her father isn't convinced of her talent, and her boyfriend can't understand why he doesn't come first in her life. But Maggie—gifted and determined—will let nothing stand in her way. "Delightful...Karen Strickler Dean has shown how tough, how demanding a life devoted to dance can be...points out the importance of family and friends." *Los Angeles Times*

BETWEEN DANCES:
Maggie Adams Eighteenth Summer   79285/$2.25
In this sequel to MAGGIE ADAMS, DANCER, Maggie has just graduated from high school and is sure to win an apprenticeship with the San Francisco City Ballet Company. But on her 18th birthday, her hopes are devastated; her close friend, Lupe, wins the only female opening. However, Lupe leaves the ballet company to marry the man she loves—a decision Maggie can't understand. But when Maggie finds herself faced with a similar choice, she realizes just how difficult it is to make the decision between love and dance.

MARIANA   78345/$1.95
15-year-old Mariana is growing into a strong and graceful dancer. But a handsome piano student comes into her life, and Mariana finds herself torn between two dreams when she falls in love for the first time—and risks undoing all her years of rigorous ballet training.

Dean 5-82